The Governess' Debut

WENDY MAY ANDREWS

~~~

Sparrow Ink
www.sparrowdeck.com
~~~

The governess must charm both the spoiled child and the haughty earl.

Orphaned and destitute, gently born Felicia Scott must find a way to keep a roof over her head. No longer able to enter the Marriage Mart, but also not of the servant class, the only option is to find a position as governess.

After his spoiled, seven year old daughter has sent off three governesses in the 18 months since her mother died, the Earl of Standish doubts the young, inexperienced Miss Scott could possibly manage the position. Since he's desperate and she comes so highly recommended, the earl agrees to give her a chance. Much to everyone's amazement, the beautiful, young governess succeeds where the others had failed. The entire household benefits from the calm, including the jaded earl.

How does he overcome his arrogance to see his governess' true value?

ISBN - 978-1-989634-20-2

www.wendymayandrews.com

Dedication

In this book, Felicia Scott has suffered through the loss of her parents and the betrayal of her brother but she manages to keep a positive outlook on life. Your perspective is a choice. So this book is for everyone who chooses happy.

Acknowledgements

My gorgeous cover is from GermanCreative on Fiverr.

My excellent edits are by Julie Sherwood. Any remaining flaws are my doing.

The basis for every happily ever after I write is from the positive background I have thanks to my fantastic Mum & Dad and the wonderful present I have with my own hero. So I thank the three of them for my happy life

Chapter One

Lord Victor Astley, the fifth Earl of Standish, was surprised by his undisciplined reaction when the young woman was announced. He was always in control of himself and his environment. It was decidedly out of character for him to be unnerved by the presence of a young woman in his library.

"Miss Felicia Scott to see you, my lord," Alfred, the earl's aging butler, had announced in even tones, not revealing anything about his own reaction to the elegant young woman who had been recommended to fill the post of governess to the earl's hoyden of a daughter.

The earl nodded to her from behind his desk, not bothering to come around to bow over her hand. "Thank you, Alfred. Please see that a tea tray is brought in momentarily."

Felicia dipped into a respectful, deep curtsy, forgetting for a moment that her new position in the servant class did not require the varying degrees of courtesy. When it did cross her mind, she dismissed the thought, surmising accurately that the haughty-looking earl would consider the extra depth to be his due.

Felicia had made every effort to appear as serious and trustworthy as possible. Her sober gown of brown worsted material was perfect for whatever activities she would be involved in while chasing after a seven-year-old child. Realizing she looked quite young, she had scraped her thick, curly, brown hair into the severest hairstyle she could manage, hoping it lent her an air of maturity.

Of course, in her innocence, she was unaware of the things that were impossible to hide – her obvious breeding was evident in her proudly erect carriage. Intelligence shone from her wide, shining, green eyes as she glanced around the earl's handsomely appointed library.

Her own governess had done her best to prepare her, but since this was the first time Felicia had applied for a position, she was somewhat uncertain as to proper protocol. The earl was still gazing at her with a rather arrested expression on his severe but still handsome face, so she surmised he was waiting for her to say something.

"Thank you for agreeing to see me, my lord."

The earl blinked away his momentary inertia. Despite the glowing recommendations he had received, it was obvious to him she would be impossible for the position. He was uncomfortable with the strange reaction he felt in her presence; besides, she was much too young. There was no way she would be able to control his daughter. Nonetheless, he supposed he still had to interview her.

"How do you know the countess?" he asked politely after resuming his seat.

"I met your mother through my governess, Miss Miranda Masters. They know each other from their involvement with the foundling hospital. When I came to stay with Miranda she took me with her to help there, and Lady Standish was very kind."

The earl's eyebrows rose slightly at this statement. He loved his mother dearly, but it was rare for him to hear her described as kind. She was a proud, stiff woman from his experience. But she did seem to enjoy her time spent at the foundling hospital, so he supposed there must be another side to her with which he was unfamiliar. He decided no further comment on the subject of his mother was required.

Still perusing the papers in front of him and not quite looking at her, he continued with his questions. "It seems you have been well educated. I see you attended the School for Young Ladies in Bath. I had thought to send Penelope there when she is of age."

Felicia surprised the earl by jumping in with an enthusiastic endorsement. "The school is quite lovely. I missed home dreadfully at first, of course, but I would not trade my time there for anything. Lady Penelope would be lucky to have the experience."

"Were you a scholarship student? I know some schools offer assistance to very advanced students."

Feeling her cheeks warm with embarrassment, Felicia answered truthfully. "No, my lord. I did well enough in my studies to be sufficiently qualified to teach your daughter her lessons, but my tuition was paid by my father."

"Hmm," was his noncommittal response before continuing. "You mentioned your governess, Miss Masters. She writes some glowing recommendations of you." Turning his coldly piercing gaze upon her finally, he asked, "How do you come to find yourself seeking a position as governess in my household, if you were raised in circumstances where your parents could afford your own governess and send you to finishing school? Is this some sort of ruse to compromise me?"

A wave of hot colour washed over Felicia, followed by her face turning a sickly pale, and she leapt to her feet to defend herself. "This is no ruse, my lord. Have you never heard of people falling on hard times? It is really none of your business why I need a position."

Realizing losing her temper with a potential employer was not going to help her get a job, Felicia tried to regain control of her emotions. She resumed her seat and continued in softer tones. "I am qualified, and I come highly recommended. Is that not sufficient?"

The earl did not seem to think so. "You are rather young."

"I am almost twenty, my lord," she answered with a defiant lift of her chin and a proud dignity in her bearing.

Lord Standish could not restrain his mocking grin at her words and attitude, which caused his visitor to again flush to the roots of her severe hairstyle. He continued, "I love my daughter, but she is a handful. This is my third time to be interviewing for governesses since my wife died eighteen months ago. What makes you think you would be able to handle her?"

Feeling on more stable ground, Felicia answered calmly. "According to my own governess, I was a handful at your daughter's age. Miranda did a remarkable job of holding onto her patience with me, and she managed to prepare me for life at school. I am uniquely qualified to be governess to your daughter, as I have been in exactly her position myself."

Again the earl's eyebrows rose sardonically. "You were an earl's daughter whose mother died when you were six?"

"No, my father was merely a baron, but I am an orphan now." Hearing the tremble in her voice, Felicia cleared her throat delicately before continuing. "I was actually referring to my being a rambunctious child with a governess. I think I should be able to figure out how to counteract any of her efforts to outsmart me, since she should not be able to come up with anything I did not try myself at her age."

Lord Standish had to admit to the sense in her reasoning, but he still felt hesitant about having the pretty young woman on his staff. He was about to voice objections, but his daughter barging into the room closely followed by his harried-looking housekeeper interrupted them.

"I am so sorry for interrupting, my lord. I just could not stop her, and really I have so many things to do. I think it would be better if one of the young maids were to try to keep an eye on her." The aging housekeeper looked to be at the end of her endurance. The earl was about to speak in irritation, but they were both brought up short by the interaction between the little lady and the earl's visitor.

"Who are you?" demanded the young child imperiously.

"My name is Felicia, what is yours?"

"I am Lady Penelope," she declared with pride.

"I am happy to meet you, Lady Penelope," answered Felicia, keeping a straight face and serious voice with a degree of difficulty. "Was the matter terribly urgent that you wished to discuss with your father? He and I were having a discussion, but if your matter is urgent, I could wait for a moment."

The little girl blinked at Felicia while suspicion and hesitance warred on her face. She realized her father would not like to be interrupted while in his library, but she could not make herself wait.

"It *is* a terribly important matter," she declared.

"Should I leave?" Felicia asked curiously.

"Are you going to be my latest governess?"

"Possibly."

"Then you need to know what I think, too. I do not want to read!" With that statement, the young lady crossed her arms belligerently while sticking her nose in the air in a defiant manner, and her firm little chin, so like her father's, took a stubborn position.

Felicia just barely managed to contain her mirth. "You do not wish to read?" she asked incredulously. "Why ever not? Reading is one of the very best activities there is."

Penelope looked at Felicia with surprise and suspicion. The earl watched the interchange with intense curiosity. If the young woman could manage his daughter, the job would most definitely have to be hers.

"I don't want to read!" Penelope repeated even more insistently without adding any more explanation.

"But you still have not said why. Surely you must have a reason to refuse." At this point Felicia was actually finding the obnoxious child rather endearing. Miranda had told her the earl's daughter was seven years old. Felicia did not have an overabundance of experience with children, but from what she'd seen at the foundling hospital, seven was a delightful age. Children were ready to be reasoned with and often had the most amusing explanations for everything.

"Reading is boring. Besides, my papa is an earl so I really do not see why I would need to read."

Felicia was unsure what the connection was between the two thoughts, but she decided to try a different tack instead of pursuing this particular line of reasoning.

"But your papa is a very busy man. He will not always be available to read to you. And would you not want to grow up to be as smart as him? You really need to start with reading, if you want to learn other things."

It had obviously never been suggested to Penelope that being as smart as her father was a possibility. She gazed at Felicia, suspicion and assessment clear in her eyes. "Are *you* as smart as my papa?" was the youngster's question.

With a charming, husky chuckle, Felicia cast a rueful glance at the earl. He was again struck by an awareness of her loveliness, waiting with a sense of anticipation for her answer. While her eyes twinkled with merriment, Felicia leaned toward Penelope and said in a loud whisper, "We could certainly never tell him so."

Lord Standish was taken aback by her effrontery, but had to acknowledge that clearly she must be as smart as he since she had managed to contain the scene his daughter had wanted to cause. But the young woman had not yet finished with his daughter.

"Look at all these books your papa has, do you not think it is important for an earl to know many things? As his daughter, I would think it is your responsibility to try very hard to learn many things, too. In my mind, you owe it to your position as an earl's daughter not to be ignorant."

Little Penelope had met her match. In her seven years of life, everyone had cajoled and flattered her rather than being straightforward and honest. She gazed at Felicia for a long moment.

"I'll think about it," was her noncommittal answer before she turned on her little heel, grabbed the housekeeper by the hand, and walked back out of the room.

She left silence in her wake. The earl gazed steadily at Felicia, his face impassive. Felicia smiled cheerfully, having enjoyed her encounter with the child.

"I have serious doubts that you will last very long, but as you can see, we are rather desperate.

The last governess walked out without any notice, and the rest of my staff is struggling to fill in. How soon would you be able to assume the position?" The earl had many misgivings about the wisdom of allowing this particular woman into his home, but he arrogantly determined that he would be able to manage.

"I could return within two hours with my things," Felicia calmly announced.

The earl was surprised and pleased by her reply. He stood to shake hands with his new employee. "Welcome, Miss Scott. I wish you every success."

Felicia shook the earl's hand and also dipped a quick curtsy, her own proper upbringing coming to the fore.

"When you return, the housekeeper will show you around and help you get settled, and then you can get better acquainted with Penelope over dinner."

"Thank you, my lord." Felicia turned and exited the room without a backward glance.

Chapter Two

"Oh, Miranda, the child is delightful. I can see why Lady Standish described her as a handful, but I think the poor dear is just missing her mother, and no one has seen fit to take a firm hand with her because of her loss."

"I am glad you feel optimistic about it, but are you completely sure you want to take the position? This is not the life your dear parents would have wished for you. They left me very well provided for, for which I will be eternally grateful. It would be my pleasure to keep you with me for as long as you need."

Felicia turned to her dearest friend with as wide a smile as she could muster. "Miranda, you are a dear, but I refuse to be a burden on you. My parents may have been generous with you, but I strongly doubt they set you up in a position to be able to support the both of us for the rest of our days."

After a brief sigh she continued. "After John gambled away what was left of my portion and then ran off to the Americas, leaving me to fend for myself, it was such a kindness for you to take me in. And it is a comfort for me to know your door is always open to me, but I need to make my own way in the world now."

Miranda continued to look at her former charge with concern etched on her face. "What did you think of the earl? From what I have heard, he can be rather fearsome."

"I can see why he has such a reputation. He does not strike me as someone who goes out of his way to secure anyone's good opinion. But he was polite with me. And since he has provided me with a well-paid position, I cannot speak ill of him."

"Is he as handsome as they say?" Miranda asked with a different kind of concern colouring her voice.

Felicia could not prevent the blush that quickly stained her cheeks, which caused Miranda to quickly ask, "You are not in danger of forming a *tendre* for the man, are you?"

"I think if he would smile he would be considered very handsome, but since he seems to be much inclined to frown, my heart should be quite safe. Truly, Miranda, you are worrying for nothing. As long as I can contain his daughter and do not need to run to him with complaints, I strongly doubt I will have any contact with the earl. It is highly unlikely he will be trying to socialize with his daughter's governess."

Miranda had to be satisfied with her former charges reassurance, but she continued to fret, nonetheless. She threw her arms around Felicia, giving her a fierce hug. "Promise me you will consider this your home and you will come to me with any problems or concerns."

Felicia returned the older woman's hug with equal enthusiasm. "I promise. Now you have to let me go. I gave my word I would return shortly to begin my responsibilities. The poor housekeeper looked to be at the end of her rope with trying to keep an eye on Penelope while also getting her own work done."

Miranda shook her head. "How did you turn out to be so willing to take on responsibility while your brother has none?"

Felicia laughed lightly, not wanting to dwell on the matter. "It certainly is a conundrum," she agreed.

~~~
~~~

Before long, Felicia was back at the earl's elegant home, faced with a new dilemma: should she enter by the front door or go around to the servants' entrance? A governess holds a strange position in Society – not quite a servant, but not on equal footing with her employers either. Felicia dithered a moment longer before marching up to the front door.

She was welcomed with enthusiasm by Alfred. "It is good that you returned, Miss. Lady Penelope needs you." He did not go into detail, merely summoning a footman to carry her bit of luggage while he rang for the housekeeper.

"Oh, deary, you came back!" declared the housekeeper with glee. "I am Mrs. Hill. Let me show you to your room. It is so good that you came back. Everyone will do their very best to make you comfortable, Miss."

The rather rotund older woman bustled along beside Felicia, chattering the whole way as she showed the new arrival around the extensive house. "Here is the morning room, deary, is it not lovely? The late Lady Standish had it redone just before she took sick. This is where Lady Standish, the earl's mother, comes to see Lady Penelope, so you will become familiar with this room a little. Since her ladyship passed, the countess thinks it's her place to ensure her granddaughter is getting her lessons. Lady Penelope doesn't much like it, I must warn you."

Felicia did not have much to contribute to the conversation, which was just as well, since Mrs. Hill continued on without even much of a breath. "Now, down that hallway are a couple other rooms that are, of course, kept clean and tidy, but they don't get much use nowadays, so I won't even bother showing them to you at this point. When the little lady grows up, no doubt we shall be using them a bit more. Here is where his lordship likes to take his breakfast, and next door is the dining room. And of course, you are no doubt familiar with his library, since you were just there this morning."

"This here is the door down to the kitchens. You are always welcome to go down there, but feel free to have one of the footmen or maids fetch you whatever you might need, deary. Everyone will be happy to serve you. Now, let us go up these stairs to the private quarters. You and the little lady will be on the third floor. Her ladyship, the late countess, you know, wanted to have the nursery moved downstairs to be closer to her and the earl, but it never happened before she passed, poor soul, and his lordship has not yet seen fit to have it done."

At this point, Mrs. Hill finally subsided for a moment because the climb up the few flights of stairs was making her breathless. Felicia allowed the housekeeper to catch her breath while she gazed about at the beautiful wall hangings and fixtures. It was obvious even to her untrained eye that someone with excellent taste had decorated this home. While the high ceilings and vast rooms could have been intimidating, the colour schemes and furniture choices made the spaces warm and inviting rather than off-putting. Even though she had been raised in humbler surroundings, Felicia felt comfortable in the earl's beautiful home.

They finally reached the nursery wing, and Mrs. Hill opened the door to a comfortable-looking bedchamber. Felicia realized this was to be her room, since she spied where the footman had placed her bags. She could not restrain her happy smile as she took it all in.

"This is quite lovely, Mrs. Hill. Thank you so much for showing me around. You have been most helpful. I should no doubt make haste to find Lady Penelope and get started with her."

"Oh, yes, deary, that would be wonderful. Just out this door is the nursery."

Felicia was delighted to see another door she hadn't noticed before. Her chamber had two entrances: one that entered into the nursery and one that afforded her a degree of privacy that entered into the hallway.

When they entered the main room of the nursery wing, Penelope could be seen tying a perfect bow on the rope she had wound around the maid who had been assigned the task of watching over the earl's recalcitrant daughter. The maid appeared wilted but that quickly changed to thrilled upon seeing more responsible adults entering the room. Penelope turned her back on them disdainfully. "Oh, it's you," she said with an obvious lack of enthusiasm.

Felicia contained her mirth at the sight before her. Obviously the child was in desperate need of being taken firmly in hand.

"Hello, Penelope."

"I am *Lady* Penelope," the hoyden emphasized.

"Well, you are not currently acting like a lady, so I really see no need to address you as such."

Penelope gazed at her new governess with wide, fascinated eyes, not prepared with a ready answer to this surprising statement.

"Now, Penelope, please untie the maid. I'm sorry I don't know your name." Felicia addressed the maid in a calm, warm tone, helping the young woman retain her composure.

"It's Mary, Miss. Thank you, Miss."

"Penelope, Mary has things she needs to be doing. I saw a lovely park on my way here. I was thinking we could go for a little walk before we have our supper."

Penelope did a little dance of delight. "We could go to the park?" she asked. "My grandmother always says I should be kept indoors, that it isn't healthy for a young lady to play at the park."

Felicia nearly winced at this, not wanting to put a wrong foot so early in her employment, but she wasn't about to go back on her word to the child either. She wracked her brain momentarily before answering briskly. "Well, your grandmother is not here, and it is a lovely, warm day, perfect for spending a bit of time at the park. Perhaps your grandmother was referring to winter as an unhealthy time for a young lady to play out of doors. Or she may not have wanted your nose to freckle, so be sure to find a hat before we go."

Penelope was quick to do as she had been instructed in this instance, unwinding the rope she had made from her sashes in order to tie up the young maid.

"Thank you, Miss. You arrived just in the nick of time." Mary was nearly overcome by her gratitude.

"Penelope, I think you owe Mary an apology."

Penelope was now shocked. No one had ever expected such a thing of her before. "Why?"

"Well, for one thing, it was very unkind to tie her up, but also, look at the mess you have made of all your sashes. It is going to be a great deal of work for her to straighten those out for you."

"But that's her job," the youngster declared, still puzzled, "and I am the earl's daughter."

Felicia couldn't help herself and was unable to contain her mirth this time. "I have a distinct feeling I am going to be hearing this explanation for any number of behaviours."

Mrs. Hill and Mary watched this exchange with avid interest. Since her mother had died, no one had been able to control Penelope. Most of the staff looked upon her with varying degrees of terror.

Ignoring the suspicion that this entire conversation was going to be repeated multiple times amongst the servants, Felicia kept her attention focused squarely on the child.

"I would say it is precisely *because* you are the earl's daughter that you owe Mary an apology. Can you imagine your grandmother tying up one of her maids with a rope of sashes?"

This logic struck Penelope forcefully, and she actually giggled at the image Felicia had drawn.

"No, but I didn't hurt her."

"Well, that's good, but she might have been scared. Have you ever been tied up?"

"No."

"Were you planning to leave her by herself like that?"

Penelope hung her head, finally beginning to see the shame of what she had done. Felicia pressed the point home. "Do you think you would find it a bit scary to be tied up and left by yourself?"

Penelope merely nodded.

"So, what do you think you should say to Mary?"

The little girl ran to the maid and threw her arms around her waist. "I'm sorry, Mary. I promise not to tie you up again."

Mary was delighted with the turn of events but was at a loss for words, gazing helplessly at Mrs. Hill. The housekeeper understood what had just been accomplished but was also at a loss as to what to say.

"That was excellent, Penelope. Now as soon as we straighten up the room here, you and I can be off for our walk, and Mrs. Hill and Mary can go about their business." Felicia covered the awkward silence and kept control of the situation.

It was clear the youngster had never been asked to help clean up her own mess before, but in her current subdued frame of mind, she pitched in gamely. The three adults and small child quickly had the room sorted.

Felicia soon tied a pretty straw hat on top of the young lady's curls and the two of them set off in fine humour, leaving a stunned silence in their wake.

"Well if that don't beat all." For once the usually verbose housekeeper had nothing else to say. The two servants made their way down to the kitchens where they regaled the rest of the staff with a word by word description of what had taken place with the new governess and the young lady. Much to Mrs. Hill's satisfaction, the entire household was agog with the news that someone had finally taken charge of Lady Penelope. She made sure to tell the earl's valet all about it in the hopes that he would see fit to divulge the entire scene to Lord Standish while he was assisting him to dress for his evening's entertainments.

~~~
~~~

Meanwhile, blissfully unaware of the stir she had caused, Felicia skipped along with Penelope, listening as the youngster told her a story about the last time she had been out of the house. Still unused to London, Felicia had been momentarily distracted by all the sights around her, but she dragged her attention back to Penelope's tale.

"Excuse me, Lady Penelope, I am sorry to interrupt you, but are you saying it has been two *months* since you were out of doors?" She made every effort to keep the horror out of her voice, but she feared she had not quite succeeded when Penelope stopped walking and looked at her with a reproachful stare.

"I *told* you my grandmother said it is unhealthy for young ladies."

"Yes, you did tell me that. I shall have to discuss this with your father. In the meantime, we are here now, so we should make the best of it lest we be told we cannot return."

Grinning at one another, they began a vigorous game of chase that was closely followed by various other games. The two girls were enjoying themselves to such an extent that the time quickly passed. Felicia was dismayed to see the daylight beginning to wane, but she quickly called a halt to the games. Grabbing Penelope's hand, she walked as briskly as possible back to the earl's home. All the playing had worn the little girl out, so while they were still a block away Felicia picked her up and carried her the rest of the way.

Alfred was at first dismayed at the sight of them when he answered the door. "Is all right with the young lady, Miss?"

"Oh, yes, we have just been running ourselves ragged. Have no fear. We had a delightful time, did we not, Penelope?"

By then Penelope had been placed back on her own feet, and she looked at the butler with pink cheeks and glowing eyes, grinning from ear to ear. "It was so much fun, Alfred. We fed the ducks with crumbs Miss Felicia had in her pocket, and we played tag, and we chased butterflies. It was the best afternoon I have ever spent."

Felicia felt tears spring to her eyes at this glowing review but managed to contain herself. "But now we must look a sight, and I fear we are a wee bit late for our dinner, so we must make haste. Goodnight, Alfred."

Alfred watched in awe as the two left the room hand in hand. He too had a tale to tell the earl that evening.

Chapter Three

The next day, despite her trepidation, while Penelope was absorbed with playing with her dolls, Felicia left her in the care of one of the maids in order to seek out the earl. Alfred escorted her to the library.

"I am terribly sorry to disturb you, my lord, but I had something I wished to discuss with you."

As she entered the room, she could see the earl was deeply absorbed in some important matters. He looked up at her with impatience. When he saw who was interrupting him, his frown turned into a scowl.

Felicia paled in the face of his obvious displeasure and regretted her impulse to search him out. Unfortunately, it was too late to back down at this point. She waited for his permission to speak.

"What is it?" he demanded harshly.

She felt the blood draining from her face, and she almost stammered. "I'm sorry, my lord. I took Lady Penelope to the park yesterday, and we had a lovely time. Unfortunately, while we were there she mentioned that your lady mother would not allow it. I was raised with the belief that children should run about during the day so they have an appetite for their meals and use up their energies so they can sleep, but I would hate to gainsay you or the countess."

Felicia had become increasingly nervous the longer she talked. By the end of her explanation, she was wringing her hands together, and her voice had risen to almost a squeak. She was disgusted with herself for her lack of backbone, but it would be terrible if she were to lose her position after the very first day.

"Despite your youth and lack of experience, you came highly recommended for this position. One of the recommendations, as you know, was from my mother. Watching over Penelope and teaching her is your responsibility. From what I have heard from my household staff, you are already doing an admirable job, so for now, I will say that you are the authority on raising her. Unless I hear of something truly outlandish, you may do as you wish with her."

Felicia was happily surprised by the earl's declaration and blinked at him rather owlishly for a moment, at a loss for words.

"Thank you, my lord, Penelope will be most pleased. We really did have a lovely time at the park. We shall return again today, as long as you do not mind."

"I understand it was getting late when you returned yesterday."

Felicia flushed guiltily, forcefully reminding the earl of her youth. "Yes, my lord, it was actually starting to get dark. You see, when Penelope told me she was not allowed to go out of doors, we decided since it might be our one chance, we wanted to take advantage of what time we had. I promise not to let the time get away on me again."

Unbeknownst to her, the earl had no opinion on the matter of whether or not his daughter should be allowed to play outside. His ill-tempered frown had been a result of his own unsettled feelings with regards to the governess, not of anything she had to say. It was obvious to him that he was causing her distress, so he tried to set her at ease.

Delighted by her honesty over why they had stayed out so late the previous day, the earl could not help a short bark of laughter. It had been at least several years since he had laughed, and he was surprised to hear the sound coming from his own mouth. Ignoring the feelings coursing through him, he said his last word on the subject before dismissing her. “If you fear you might lose track of the time in the future, ensure you have a footman with you. I do not ever want to hear of you or Penelope out by yourselves if it is nearing dusk, do you understand?”

“Thank you, my lord, I will be most careful.” On those words, she curtsied herself from the room, leaving the earl in an abstracted frame of mind.

~~~

Bouncing down the hallway, grinning with delight, Felicia waved airily to the butler before gathering up her skirts and dashing up the stairs.

Alfred was still chuckling over her antics when he answered the earl’s summons. “What is the matter with you, Alfred?” Lord Standish demanded with surprise.

“Naught is wrong with me, my lord. I just find the young miss delightful. She is a breeze of fresh air that the entire household was needing, if you don’t mind my whimsy, my lord.”
~~~

The earl could not deny the truth of the older man's words, so he merely snorted in response before getting on with the business at hand.

~~~

Meanwhile, Penelope was clapping her hands in delight over the news that her governess had garnered permission for them to be allowed to go out of doors whenever the weather permitted. "Could we please go back to the park today, Felicia? It was ever so fun to feed the ducks. We could ask Cook for some bread before we go."

"That sounds like a brilliant idea. Tomorrow is time enough for your lessons to begin. Let us work out some more of our fidgets, then we will be in a better frame of mind to get on with learning tomorrow."

And so it began. The two girls set a pattern of completing lessons in the morning after breakfast and then dashing off to spend a few hours outside most afternoons, after they had eaten their lunch. They were in quite good charity with one another, and Lady Penelope was settling into a fine routine. This came to a screeching halt one afternoon late on Felicia's second week in the earl's employ, as the two of them came clamouring into the house after another one of their rambles.
~~~

“There you are, Miss. We were wondering when you would get home,” began Alfred hesitantly as he was letting them into the house.

“Were you looking for me, Alfred? Were we expected at a certain time?” Felicia asked in some confusion.

“Her ladyship, the countess, came around to visit Lady Penelope ,and we were unsure what to tell her as to when you would return.”

“Oh dear, was she terribly put out that we were not here?” Felicia asked with a worried furrow to her brow.

“She decided to wait for your return,” answered the butler.

Felicia’s eyes widened in shock. “Has she been waiting long?”

“Not overlong, Miss, but I do believe she could be getting a mite impatient by now. His lordship is with her, so you need not concern yourself. But you should make haste to present yourselves in the morning room.”

Felicia looked her young charge over, grateful that they had not been indulging in too vigorous activity that afternoon. She pulled a comb from her reticule and quickly ran it through the youngster’s curls.

"Don't make such a fuss, Felicia, I don't think my grandmother will care how neat my hair is." Penelope rarely had patience with fussing over her appearance, despite her obvious vanity.

"I disagree, Penelope, I do believe your grandmother, the countess, would expect you to present yourself to best advantage. It is a sign of respect for her position as your grandmother and as a countess. But in this instance, you may be correct, it would be better for us to be a bit messy than to keep her waiting any longer." After shaking out her own skirts, she allowed the butler to usher them into the countess' presence.

~~~

Lord Standish was quite well aware that his mother found his company to be depressing. He rarely cracked a smile and was forever out of sorts. She probably found it a struggle to spend time with her only son. On the other hand, the earl's poorly behaved daughter seemed to cause her mixed emotions. When Penelope wasn't causing the countess to wish to pull her hair out in frustration, she could be a delight to spend time with. Unfortunately, the former occasions far outweighed the latter.

The commotion at the door was a blessed distraction to both occupants of the room, who
~~~

were struggling to make desultory conversation. The earl had previously ordered a tea trolley to be brought in as soon as his daughter arrived home, so there was a great deal of activity for a few moments after Penelope bounded into her father's presence.

Felicia had dipped into a respectful curtsy as soon as she entered the room, despite her assumption that no one was paying her any attention at the moment. She was wrong in that supposition. The earl noticed everything about her, much to his chagrin. He watched with approval as she showed respect to his mother and then stood aside and watched attentively while Penelope regaled her grandmother with her own news.

The earl enjoyed watching his mother's amazement. It was obvious Lady Standish could hardly believe this was the same child. It had only been two weeks since she had last seen her granddaughter, but the time had most certainly been well spent. Obviously there was vast room for improvement, but it became apparent that the child would be pleasant to spend a visit with.

"Grandmother, we have been going every day to give bread to the ducks. They have the most darling little babies. Felicia says I mustn't make too much noise when the mama is there with her babies or she will be too afraid, but it is just so difficult to remain quiet when they are so precious. I think we should have ducks on our pond at Standish, what do you think, Papa?"

The earl looked surprised to be included in this conversation but could not help smiling at his happily exuberant daughter. "We shall have to think about it when we go home for the summer, my pet."

Turning back to the countess, Penelope continued enthusiastically. "Grandmother, Felicia says I must curtsy to you since you are a countess. Is she correct or was she just teasing me?"

Glancing momentarily at the child's governess with an ironically quirked eyebrow, the countess managed to maintain a straight face. "Yes, my darling, Miss Scott is correct, socially speaking, a countess should be curtsied to."

Penelope allowed a belligerent look to cross her face, but then she looked at Felicia. Felicia held her gaze seriously for a moment then Penelope smiled serenely at her grandmother, hiked up her skirts, and executed a rather clumsy curtsy. She grinned happily while her papa and grandmother applauded her new skill.

"You mentioned you were just coming from the park. I thought it was best that you not spend time out of doors until you return to the country." Lady Standish could not resist this censor, her son could see. The earl caught the flash of guilt on Felicia's face and was about to speak in her defense but was saved from the necessity when his daughter again launched into speech.

"Felicia thought perhaps you were concerned that I not spot up with freckles, so she says I have to always wear a hat when we are out in the sun. It is just so much fun to go out for a walk every day or go run around at the park. Felicia says I can learn more if I wear off my fidgets. I think she must be right because I feel smarter already. And it is much easier to eat the nasty porridge that Cook insists is good for me now that I run around more. Felicia says I am growing already, like a plant needs to be in the sun to grow. What do you think, Grandmother? Have I grown since you last seen me?"

The countess was unable to maintain her starchy demeanour in the face of this non sequitur; a friendly chuckle came from her before she returned gravely, "I do believe you have, my dear. I can see that Miss Scott is a most excellent companion for you."

Lady Standish smiled warmly at Felicia before turning to her son. "I am so glad that you took my advice for once."

Unable to answer this with anything other than a wry nod of his head, the earl finally turned to the miss under question. "Miss Scott, please sit down and join us for a cup of tea. I am certain the countess would love to hear more of Penelope's tales of trips to the park."

Felicia flushed with pleasure and uncertainty but took a seat as unobtrusively as possible, accepting a dainty cup of tea from the countess. She watched attentively as Penelope bounced on the settee and took mental note of further instruction the young lady would require before the next visit with the countess.

Penelope chattered away happily for several more minutes while her father and grandmother listened with waning interest. When the earl began to shift about rather restlessly, Felicia deemed it would be a good time to bring the visit to an end.

Rising gracefully, Felicia addressed Penelope. "I believe we have kept the countess quite long enough, and no doubt your father has many important duties to attend to. Let us say our farewells and adjourn to the nursery where I am sure Mary will soon be bringing us something deliciously scrumptious for our dinner."

Penelope bounded up from her seat and was about to dash from the room, but catching sight of a gesture from Felicia, she turned back to the countess and dipped down into another shaky curtsy. "Thanks for coming to visit me, Grandmama. Good-bye."

Felicia smiled at her young charge as she ran up and grabbed her hand. "Hurry up, Felicia, you promised to play a game of Fox and Geese with me later."

Felicia and Penelope left a rather stunned silence in their wake, and Lady Standish turned to her son. "That young woman has worked wonders with your child, my dear. I knew she would be a good fit for the position, but I had no idea it would work out quite that well. I never realized she had so very little to say for herself, though, I must say."

"How would you know that, Mother? Penelope barely left room for anyone else to get a word in edgewise." Lord Standish chuckled. "The governess certainly came up with a good ploy when she took to escorting the child out of doors."

"She is very pretty. Does that cause you any concern, Victor?" asked his mother with a sharp eye on his face.

Victor struggled to maintain an impassive face but could not contain the slight heat that crept into his cheeks. "It does not concern me, Mother. As long as she continues to manage Lady Penelope so well, I cannot say I care one way or the other what she looks like."

"I suppose you are correct there, my son. Well, I have dithered here long enough. I should return home, as I am promised to your sister for the evening. You should show your face around town a bit more than you do, Victor. You are turning into a recluse."

Victor managed to restrain himself from rolling his eyes but could not muster much of a smile for his mother as she took her leave. He stood respectfully until she left the room then slumped back into his chair while he smiled in reminiscence over some of his daughter's exclamations. He was relieved not to have to be so worried about her anymore. *Hopefully this good stretch holds and the governess sticks around,* he thought to himself rather pessimistically before heaving himself back to his feet and striding down the hall to immerse himself once more in his work.

Chapter Four

Felicia had to struggle to keep her attention on Penelope's lessons. Her mind kept replaying the scene in the morning room with the countess and earl the previous afternoon. She was delighted by her young charge's progress and relieved to have received the countess's approval despite countermanding her decree about not taking Penelope outside, but it was the smile on the earl's face that kept intruding into her thoughts. Prior to yesterday, Felicia had thought the earl to be a terribly stern and arrogant man and really had not thought him very handsome at all, but when he had listened to Penelope with such a soft smile on his face, it was impossible to ignore his appeal.

With a vigorous shake of her head, she forced her thoughts once more to return to the matter at hand. It was foolhardy for her to dwell on her employer's handsome face or the thrill that had shot through her when their eyes had met. Nothing could come of any warm feelings she might develop, so it was best to put it all from her mind.

"That is quite excellent, Penelope. You are making remarkable progress with your letters. I must say I am impressed. You seem to have changed your mind about learning to read."

"Yes, Felicia, I think I would like to be smart like my Papa. I still don't see that it will be of much use for me to be smart, but it should be amusing, don't you think?"

Felicia could not prevent her bark of laughter over this statement. "I am delighted that you think it will be amusing, but I am also quite sure you will find it to be very useful. Being knowledgeable will always be an asset. For young ladies, it is almost as important as being pleasant."

Penelope turned puzzled eyes to her governess' face. "Why would it be important to be pleasant? I am an earl's daughter. People will have to like me whether I am pleasant or not, won't they?"

Felicia pondered how best to answer this. Despite the improvements she had seen in the youngster, she was still a spoiled little girl with an inordinate amount of pride in her supposed position in Society.

"It is true that most will feel obliged to be nice to your face, but if you are unpleasant to be around, you can be certain that you will be a target for catty remarks behind your back. This will be particularly so when you go to finishing school."

"Well then, perhaps I shan't go away to school. I could just tell my Papa I do not wish to go," the youngster reasoned.

"But the time spent at school can be an amazing experience. You can make friends there who will be your companions for years to come. I would highly recommend the experience. Why are you so resistant to the idea of trying to be pleasant?"

Penelope lifted her little shoulders in a lopsided shrug. "It's usually difficult."

"Well, you catch more flies with sugar than vinegar."

"What does that mean?" the youngster asked with curiosity.

"People are much more drawn to sweetness than to someone who is sour like vinegar."

"But like you said, people will be drawn to me because of who my Papa is." Penelope stubbornly stuck to her original view.

Felicia sighed with the beginnings of frustration. "Penelope, did you ever think that perhaps your Papa might remarry?"

Now she had Penelope's full attention. "Why would he do that? Isn't he too old?"

"Not at all. Your father is a perfect age to remarry. And while he loves you very much, most earls really require a son to carry on their name and inherit the estate. Right now, should something terrible happen to your father, no doubt some cousin would inherit everything, and you would find yourself to be in a bit of a pickle."

Penelope wrinkled her nose while she concentrated on what her governess was trying to tell her. Felicia continued in a kind voice, sitting beside the youngster and putting her arm around her while she explained.

"If he brought home a new countess who took you in dislike, your life could become rather awkward. So just in case, you should learn to curb your persnickety ways and try to be pleasant to everyone. You could try practicing with Mary. She is a very sweet person and would be happy if you were nice to her."

"But she's my maid, Felicia," Penelope countered with confusion. "She can't really be my friend."

"Perhaps not, but if you can learn to be nice to her, you could probably be nice to anyone. And she is actually really easy to be nice to."

"I will think about it, Felicia. How do you know about this?" Penelope snuggled a bit more comfortably into Felicia's arm while awaiting further explanation.

~~~

Victor hovered just outside the door, waiting with baited breath for the rest of Felicia's explanation. He was astonished at her ability to reason with his rebellious daughter. He held himself as still as possible, not wanting to alert either occupant of the room to his presence.

"Well, for one thing I have been to the very school your father thinks would be good for you to attend, so I know how things work there. I also have had the disconcerting experience of having a major change in my circumstances. Being smart and nice were both very valuable qualities when I found myself to be homeless."
~~~

"You were homeless? What happened?" Penelope gazed at Felicia with eyes widened with shock.

"My parents died in a terrible accident sixteen months ago. We were not a terribly wealthy family, but we had a comfortable life together on my father's small estate. My brother inherited nearly everything upon my parents' death, and he was also named as the trustee for whatever I was to inherit until I married or turned twenty-five." Felicia paused in her tale. Victor could see clearly by the look of indecision on her face that she was wondering if it were wise to share this story with the child. She must have decided it would be a good lesson to the youngster because she continued.

"My foolish brother developed a taste for gambling, and he lost it all quite quickly, leaving us both penniless."

Proving she was kind in her core, Penelope hugged her governess tightly. "That's terrible, Felicia, what happened then?"

Squeezing her back, Felicia finished her story. "My brother ran away to the Americas but refused to take me with him. I think he was ashamed of what he had done and did not want me along as a reminder. He promised me he would make his fortune in the colonies and send for me, but that did me no good in the meantime. Luckily for me, my parents had provided very well for my old governess, and she was happy to take me in while I figured out what was best to be done. Then I met your grandmother and she told me about you. Now here I am, all right and tight."

"You can stay with me forever, Felicia," Penelope vowed earnestly. "Even if Papa gets a nasty new wife, we can stick together."

Felicia laughed with delight over the youngster's declaration of loyalty. "Thank you, my darling. Now enough sad tales, what say you to a trip to the park? Do you think we have learned enough for today?"

~~~

Victor realized it was time for him to take his leave if he did not wish for his presence to become known. He suspected that the governess would be embarrassed to find him listening to her story, and he couldn't think of a ready excuse for being there, so he turned on his heel to depart.

As he walked briskly away from the nursery, the earl found his admiration for his daughter's governess to be rising steadily. The pretty young woman had overcome monumental obstacles yet maintained a happy spirit. *Perhaps it is the*
~~~

optimism of youth on her side, he thought rather cynically as he struggled to push his feelings of attraction toward her far to the back of his mind. He reached his library, shut the door firmly, and ignored the happy sounds as Penelope and Felicia bade farewell to the butler on their way out the door.

Moments later, despite his best efforts, the earl could not resist asking Alfred where the girls had said they would be going.

"My lord, my apologies. I did not foresee the need to ask Miss Felicia where she and my lady Penelope were headed. I see now that it would be advisable to be conscious of their whereabouts. I do know they had bread for the ducklings, and I believe they have previously mentioned that the ducks are living in Hyde Park."

"Do not trouble yourself, Alfred. Miss Scott seems to be highly proficient. I am sure no ill will befall them. But in the future, as you say, it would be advisable for the household to be aware of their plans lest we need to find them for some reason or another."

The earl returned to his library feeling rather melancholy for a number of moments before he threw caution to the wind and summoned a footman to send round to the stables for his horse to be readied. He then bolted up to his bedchamber and changed into more appropriate attire.

"It is a dashed fine day for a ride, would you not say?" he remarked to his startled valet. The well-trained servant did not point out that his lordship so rarely went riding, especially not in the middle of the day, and merely helped the earl to ease into his form-fitting coat.

As the earl descended once more to the foyer, the butler too had the good sense not to comment on the unprecedented nature of the earl's excursion, merely wishing him a good ride. "Should I know where you are heading, my lord?" Alfred thought to ask.

"I am not a female of the house, Alfred. I do not need to apprise anyone of my whereabouts," the earl haughtily answered, despite the twinkle shining in his eyes. He left the house feeling as though there were a bounce in his step, and he fought with a desire to whistle a jaunty tune, knowing that his faithful servants were already regarding him as though he had turned into a stranger. He decided he didn't much care what they thought and bounded toward the stables.

~~~
~~~

Felicia and Penelope were blissfully unaware of the earl's failed struggle against his urge to see them. They were happily tossing chunks of bread to the greedy ducks and swans on the slow moving serpentine in the middle of Hyde Park. When they had emptied their bag of every last crumb, Felicia finally convinced Penelope to step away from the riverbank. Despite how much they both enjoyed the antics of the ducklings, Felicia could not be completely at ease while her charge was so close to the edge. She suspected the earl would not look at their excursions in such a positive light were he to know how close his daughter had been to tumbling into the murky water on a number of occasions.

As though her thoughts had conjured him, Felicia glanced around and saw a rider heading in their direction who bore a striking resemblance to Lord Standish.

"Penelope, is that your father by any chance?"

Distracted, Penelope barely glanced up at the question. "My father never goes to the park, Felicia, so I wouldn't think so."

"I am serious, Penelope. Look over there. I am quite certain that is the earl."

Penelope looked in the direction indicated, and her eyes widened in surprise. She then began hopping up and down, waving her arms and yelling, "Papa, Papa, we're over here!" thus bringing a fiery blush to her governess' cheeks at the unwanted attention being drawn to them by the aristocratic crowd.

"Penelope Astley, that is no way for a lady to behave," Felicia hissed.

"But he will never find us if I don't yell," Penelope answered with all reasonableness.

"Perhaps he is not looking for us and merely wishes to have a quiet ride in the park on this beautiful day." Felicia was so mortified that she could not look in the earl's direction, so she was unaware that he had heard his daughter's summons and was now heading straight toward them.

Penelope did not hesitate to point it out. "He is coming right this way, so I do think he was looking for me. So you see, it is good that I yelled."

"Penelope, you little hoyden, I could have heard you all the way at our house," the earl announced as soon as he reached them. "I thought you were working on your manners."

Felicia took this as a reprimand toward her and stammered out an apology. "I am so sorry, my lord. It is my fault. I pointed you out to her, and she was so excited to see you. She thought perhaps you were looking for us, and she wanted to ensure you did not miss her."

The earl could not resist laughing at her disjointed apology. "My daughter's behaviour has improved drastically since your arrival, Miss Scott, have no fear. I do not lay the blame for this particular outburst at your feet. It should just be apparent to you that you still have a great deal of work before you."

There was a momentary pause while both girls digested this with vastly different reactions. Felicia's flush turned to one of proud delight, while Penelope stuck her lower lip out in a belligerent sulk. Fortunately, the earl nipped this in the bud with his next words.

"But in this case, my darling brat, you were correct in that I was looking for you. I would like to think my powers of deduction are sufficient that I would have been able to find you without your very loud summons, but I particularly wanted to know if you and Miss Scott would like to accompany me to Gunther's for a little treat this afternoon."

Penelope's face undertook a radical change. All smiles, the young girl actually did a little dance of glee. "Oh, Papa, that would be absolutely marvellous. Felicia and I have walked past there a few times, and I must admit that I pressed my nose to the window, even though she told me it was very ill bred behaviour. We wanted to go in, but Felicia said she didn't have the coins for any of the treats in there. I am quite certain you have enough coins for all of us, right Papa?"

The earl was watching his daughter's governess closely throughout this entire conversation and began to worry about the poor young woman's health. Her face continued to glow bright red over his daughter's latest statement. He realized she was embarrassed over her lack of funds. Victor was unsure how to set the poor girl at ease since it was his own fault for not telling her to apply to him for spending money for his daughter's use. Since he had overheard her explanation to Penelope about her newly straightened circumstances, he now understood that it was no doubt pride that motivated her embarrassment over her lack of money. He decided to address the matter at another time and just ignored her discomfort, hoping she would quickly get over it.

"You are quite right, sweet pea. I have more than enough funds to treat two lovely ladies to some ices or cakes. Shall we proceed?"

Feeling embarrassed and not wanting to intrude on the earl's time with his daughter, Felicia tried to excuse herself. "Perhaps I should head home, and you could enjoy Penelope's company without my presence."

"No, Felicia, you must come too. How will I ever be able to pick which treat is the best without you to advise me?" Penelope reached for her friend's hand and held on tight.

The earl quickly added his own encouragement. "I fully intended for both of you to join me, Miss Scott. It would not be the same without you."

Still uncertain but unable to resist the lure of the prospect of seeing the confectioners shop from the inside, Felicia accepted the invitation with grace. "Thank you, my lord, that would be quite lovely," she acquiesced in soft tones before turning to Penelope with excitement.

"It shall be so hard to discern which one we could smell from the street. Remember the other day when our tongues were just dripping from how sweet it smelled?"

"Maybe we should just order one of each thing," Penelope suggested with a giggle.

"No, then we would get sick in our stomachs and the entire experience would be ruined. I say we should each order one thing, and then each have half of the other's. That way we can savor both and enjoy the experience without making ourselves ill. There is always next time to try something else," was Felicia's reasonable answer.

"But what if there is no next time?" whined Penelope.

"Have no fear, sweet pea, I will ensure there is a next time." The earl's amusement was evident as he stepped in to help negotiate the process. "Now hurry along, girls, or all the best treats will be taken."

This prompted more giggles from his companions, but they did as he bade and hastened their steps. The trio no doubt drew a bit of speculative attention as they exited the park by way of Stanhope Gate with the earl's large horse bringing up the rear of their party. After a brief pause in the mews behind Lord Standish's house, they proceeded along Charles Street and came out onto Berkeley Square.

"I have an idea. Why do we not go in, make our selections, and then have the waiter bring our treats over to the park across the street so we can continue to take advantage of this lovely day?"

"What a marvellous idea, my lord." Felicia knew Penelope would love to be out of doors, and she would likewise enjoy the opportunity to gaze about at all the finely dressed people coming and going on the busy street.

Both Felicia and Penelope had to struggle to keep their jaws from dropping open as they gazed about the rather opulent interior of the confectionery. Their noses were practically quivering from the various enticing smells. The menu was extensive, and they dithered a few moments, trying to decide.

“Oh, Penelope, how will we ever decide? I am quite certain your father will lose all patience with us if we do not hurry up. I am torn between a sugarplum and the orange and lemon ice. What do you think you would like to try?”

“I think I would like a taste of the jasmine ice cream. I really think you must have the ice, Felicia, since it is growing quite warm. Your cheeks look pink, so you must be hot.” The innocent child did not realize how embarrassed Felicia was over receiving the earl’s attention, causing Felicia’s cheeks to turn a brighter shade of pink.

Felicia could not contain her laughter despite her discomfiture. “I do believe you are correct, Penelope. That decides it, ices for us both.”

After the earl placed the order, the three of them traipsed across the street and found the perfect spot to sit under the wide reaching bows of an accommodating maple tree.

"This was a terrific idea, Papa. However did you know how much we wished to enjoy a treat?"

The earl laughed and tweaked his daughter's nose playfully. "I know you, my darling daughter. You would always enjoy a treat." He paused for a moment before honesty forced him to acknowledge, "But I must admit, I had no idea the degree of enthusiasm my suggestion would engender. I am happy to oblige."

Felicia was so enjoying Lord Standish's company that she could barely look at him. She recalled her conversation with Melinda about how the earl could be considered handsome if only he would smile. It seemed this afternoon he never ceased that activity. It had a most distressing impact on the rhythm of the poor young governess' heart.

Penelope kept up a steady stream of commentary and questions, so there were no awkward silences until the waiter arrived with their treats. The earl had simply requested a cup of strong tea for himself, but he was happy to observe as his two companions tucked enthusiastically into their bowls.

After a few moments of companionable silence while they each savoured their treats and indulged themselves in their own thoughts, Penelope was the first to break back into speech.

"That was so nice, Papa, thank you."

The earl was impressed with his daughter's improving manners and could not help looking at her governess, since he knew her to be the source of her instructions. Meeting Felicia's eye, he felt a current of awareness arrow through him before he could tear his gaze away, returning his attention to Penelope.

"When can we come again?" Penelope's question managed to break the strange spell holding the adults in thrall as they burst into uproarish laughter, relieving their nervous tensions.

"Soon, sweet pea, I promise. Now, what do you say we head back home? I have a few things I need to work on before I go on some appointments this evening."

"Oh, my lord, I pray you, do not allow us to detain you any longer." Felicia was mortified at this reminder of how busy the earl was. "Lady Penelope and I shall be just fine on our own. "

When the earl made as if to protest, she hastened to add, "If you go on ahead of us, we can dawdle along at whatever pace we see fit, stopping to admire whatever shall catch our eye. If we accompany you, since you have places to be, we shall have to scurry along in your wake."

The earl grinned at her charming choice of words, but did agree with the wisdom of them. "Normally, a gentleman must see his guests home safely before leaving them to their own devices, but in this case, I do see how there is an element of sense in what you say."

Turning to his daughter, he reminded her, "You mind whatever Miss Scott says, young lady," before reminding the governess, "Please ensure you are home long before dark."

"Yes, m'lord." Felicia dropped a brief curtsy at this before clasping Penelope's hand and walking away from the earl.

Victor was surprised to feel as though the young chit had dismissed him, but then he saw there were some squirrels chattering in a copse of trees and Penelope's attention was engaged. He smiled admiringly at the picture the two girls presented before he shook his head of his whimsical thoughts and strode off toward Charles Street.

Chapter Five

Several days passed during which Penelope continued to advance in her lessons and blossom under the warm but firm tutelage of the kind and serious young governess. Felicia was surprised on occasion to glance up from whichever textbook they were perusing to see the earl hovering at the door. Each time she caught sight of his assessing gaze upon her, she felt a bolt of awareness before he turned and strode away down the hall. He never engaged her in conversation and did not repeat the previously unprecedented action of following them to the park.

Felicia had been gratified at his thoughtfulness toward her and Penelope when Mrs. Hill had told her about the earl's decree that she be given access to an allowance of funds for whatever expenses she may incur on behalf of the earl's daughter. She had fleetingly wondered why he had not told her of it himself on one of the many occasions he stopped by the nursery. Due to her lack of experience, she thought it was usual for an employer to check on his children and their caregiver. It was not, and the earl was constantly berating himself for feeling so drawn to the governess. He had never had trouble avoiding the nursery in times past.

So it was with dismay that Victor heard his mother demanding that Felicia be summoned that afternoon when she stopped in for a brief visit with Penelope.

"Alfred, please ensure that Miss Scott accompanies Lady Penelope when she comes to share tea with me," the countess decreed, leaving the earl no way around it.

"Mother, we do not require the services of the governess while we visit with the child," he said, unable to resist the attempt.

"But she is such a lovely young woman and has such an excellent effect on our little Penelope that I feel we really must include her. No doubt she would appreciate some adult conversation for once."

When Victor made no comment aside from a dubious expression on his face, his mother continued. "You do realize she used to be a squire's daughter, or perhaps a baron. She used to move about the lower levels of Society out in whatever small town she was from. Despite her excellent education, she probably did not spend this much time with children, since she was a child herself."

"I still do not see why this means we must take tea with her," the earl complained superciliously. He did not wish to admit even to himself that he truly had no objection to spending time with her other than to avoid the uncomfortable feelings of attraction that arose in her presence. They had exchanged few words in actual conversation other than during her interview. Most of his observations were of her interaction with his daughter. That was enough for him to see her stellar qualities.

The conversation between mother and son was quickly terminated when they heard the giggles and whispers by the door scant seconds before Penelope bounded through. She came to an abrupt halt and dipped into a much-improved curtsy. Upon completing her deep show of respect with a grin upon her cherubic face, she ran to give her grandmother a quick hug.

Unused to such displays of affection, the countess was taken aback at first, but quickly returned the youngster's embrace. Over

Penelope's head she threw a quick smile at the governess who was hovering near the door.

"Come in, Miss Scott, and take a seat. Alfred will be bringing in the tea trolley momentarily."

Felicia was gratified by Lady Standish's condescension but was intimidated by the earl's thunderous expression. She gracefully settled into a small chair as far from him as possible without appearing rude. Victor took note of the action, as well as her averted face, and correctly interpreted it to mean she wished to avoid contact with him. Perversely, this caused him amusement and made him wish to converse with her.

While Penelope was regaling her grandmother with tales of her activities over the past week, Victor endeavoured to engage Felicia in conversation.

"It is good of you to join us, Miss Scott," he began, leaning a bit forward in his chair to make eye contact.

Felicia's startled eyes flew to meet his own, bewilderment clearly etched on her face. "Alfred said I was summoned, my lord. I trust I am not intruding."

"No, no, I am in earnest. I swear there was no sarcasm behind my statement. It *is* good that you could join us," he insisted. "My mother reminded me you might be sadly in want of adult conversation."

Felicia blushed rosily but shook her head in denial. "Penelope is a lovely conversationalist, my lord, and I dearly enjoy her company. But a nice cup of tea will be undeniably welcome," she added shyly.

Victor gave up his pretence at starchiness and moved over to a settee closer to her seat in order to carry on the conversation without talking around Penelope and the countess. Felicia's blush deepened at his nearness. Despite her attention given primarily to Penelope, the countess' eyes sharpened on her son as he leaned toward the governess. He ignored his mother.

"I failed to ask you, is this your first time to be in the capital, Miss Scott?"

"Yes, my lord. My father travelled to the city periodically, but I had yet to come until now. My mother had always wished to bring me for the Season but..." Felicia broke off that thought with a nervous shrug and an uncomfortable smile.

The earl took pity on her, filling the growing silence between them with another question. "So now that you have been here for a while, what do you think of our fine city?"

This must have been exactly the right question, for her eyes took on a delightful gleam, and she broke into animated exclamation. "I love it, my lord. The hustle and bustle of busy, beautiful people is so exciting. I know this particular part of town is quite unique, but I enjoy looking at all the elegant houses and the handsome horses as they prance past. And, my lord, I must thank you for putting funds at our disposal. Penelope and I have been able to venture a bit further afield. We have visited a couple of museums this week, which I think will be particularly good for her education. Was it not generous of the king to give over the use of one of his residences to house Lord Elgin's collections?"

Victor couldn't help smiling as she paused to ask this question. In her enthusiasm, she bore a marked resemblance to Penelope, although her exclamations were in much more contained tones. He saw she was looking at him expectantly and realized she was awaiting his response.

"Oh, yes, prodigious generous," he was forced to say.

"Have you been to see the collection yourself, my lord?"

"I have not yet had the pleasure," he answered with a feigned degree of regret. The earl did not feel it necessary to inform the young woman that he thought it was ridiculous that Lord Elgin had seen fit to bring half of the relics of the Ottoman Empire to litter up the streets of London.

Perhaps sensing his thoughts, or maybe just being of like mind, Felicia wrinkled her nose in thought, causing the earl's gaze to sharpen on her attractive face. "Do you not think the people of those places might object to his lordship making off with their artefacts, my lord?" she asked with a worried note.

Surprised by her astute observation, the earl decided to probe further. "Have you been listening to Byron, Miss Scott?"

"No, my lord. Did he have a comment on the subject?" she asked innocently.

"Byron refuses to visit the museum, as he has declared Lord Elgin to be nothing but a looter."

Felicia could barely contain her gasp. "But did the earl not have permission, my lord? It would hardly have gone unnoticed when he was dismantling and shipping all those pieces. They are far from tiny. It is not as though he were able to smuggle them out inside his coat," she exclaimed with reason, despite her own misgivings over the propriety of the matter.

The earl looked amused at the thought that crossed his mind. "I would love to hear you try to explain that to Byron."

Felicia blushed with embarrassment. "I beg leave to doubt that I will ever find myself in the position of discussing the matter with either Lord Byron or the earl. But whether or not it was a good idea to bring the pieces all the way here, I cannot regret that he did, since I will never have the opportunity to travel to see where they came from, and I wholeheartedly enjoyed viewing them."

The earl was saved from further comment by the arrival of the butler wheeling the tea trolley. There was the momentary bustle of activity while the countess poured for everyone. Even Penelope had her own cup, generously diluted with milk, which she balanced precariously while looking to her governess for guidance. Felicia smiled encouragingly at her. Ever observant, the countess saw the small exchange and was heartened.

"Miss Scott, my darling Penelope has been telling me of all your doings this week. It seems to me that the two of you have been very active."

Felicia smiled once more at Penelope before answering the countess' observation. "'Tis true, m'lady. We have had a wonderful week. The weather has been amazingly cooperative, and Penelope has been very quick about her lessons every day, which has allowed us plenty of time to wander about. Neither she nor I have seen much of London before, so we are discovering everything together."

The countess nodded her approval. "Some of the children at the foundling hospital have been asking about you." Lady Standish had meant this as a compliment, so was therefore taken aback by the sudden tears that sprang to Felicia's eyes.

"Oh, the poor dears, I did not think to go bid them farewell before I settled in here. How remiss of me. They have had to endure so much loss in their lives. it was truly thoughtless of me to not have thought that they would miss me." Felicia was obviously becoming distressed over the subject, but her companions did not know what to say.

Penelope took exception to her governess' words. She put her cup down and ran to Felicia, forcing her way onto her lap. "But you have me now. You don't need anyone else, especially not foundling children."

With a watery chuckle, Felicia gave her young charge a warm squeeze. "I know, my darling. And it is not that I need those children, it is just that they have so little, and they are so appreciative of everything. Perhaps when I go to visit my dear friend Melinda, she and I could go and visit them."

"I could go with you, Felicia," Penelope offered, unsure if she should be jealous of her governess wanting to visit other children.

"That is such a lovely offer, my dear, but I am not certain of the wisdom of that." Felicia managed to pull herself together and realized the need to tread carefully. "Now, let us put the matter aside for the moment and enjoy the rest of our visit with your grandmother. I think you have yet to tell her about the kittens we found in the attic."

Thus diverted, Penelope wriggled off her lap and returned to her grandmother with yet another story.

The earl was regarding her steadily, so Felicia felt the urge to speak. "I apologize, my lord, I did not think how Penelope would react."

"No apologies are necessary, I assure you, Miss Scott. For one thing, Penelope must realize at some point that she is not the only person in the world, and for another, you are perfectly entitled to your feelings. They are rather noble feelings, at that. It might actually be good for Penelope to see the circumstances of those less fortunate than her."

Felicia tried to keep her face impassive, but her feelings must have been displayed because the earl paused in his musings to ask her quietly, "Do you disagree, Miss Scott?"

"No, my lord, I wholeheartedly agree that it would be good for Penelope to be aware that her privileged circumstances are rare in this world. But I do not think the foundling children are a spectacle to be observed, and I think it would be hurtful to them to bring a privileged child into their midst. They understand and accept the charity they receive from ladies like the countess, but a child of an age with them would be another thing altogether. Thank you for thoughtfully offering that I could venture there with Penelope, but I believe it would be best if I wait until I can accompany Melinda."

The earl was left with the strange sensation that he had been reprimanded by his beautiful, young governess and initially bristled at the thought until he realized that she was correct. He had failed to consider the children's feelings. Perhaps he, too, needed a lesson on appreciation of his own privileged status.

When the time had come for Felicia to take Penelope back to the nursery she thanked the countess politely for including her in the invitation to tea. She then curtsied elegantly, and whisked the youngster back upstairs after she, too, had executed her curtsy to her grandmother.

As they were leaving the room, Lord and Lady Standish smiled to hear Penelope chatter on about the kittens. "Please, Felicia, could we go back up to the attic to look at them once more before we go back to the schoolroom? Don't you think we should make sure the mama cat has enough to eat? It must be a big job to look after all those babies."

~~~

Felicia's tinkling laugh was the last they heard as the two girls ascended the stairs. The countess turned to her son.

"What a delightful visit that was, Victor. I do believe our darling has turned a corner." She paused to reflect upon her own statement before continuing. "You have not forgotten about my plans to host a dinner party here next week, have you?"

"No, my lady, I have not forgotten, try as I might," he replied dryly.

"Why would you wish to forget?" she puzzled.
~~~

"So I would have a legitimate reason for being absent on the prescribed day," was the droll answer.

"Oh dear, are you truly dreading it to that degree? I suppose I should apologize for intruding, but this did used to be my home, and it is ever so much more suited for the size of gathering I wish to hold."

"Mother, this is still your home, and you are to feel free to make use of it whenever you wish. I told you that when you moved out."

"But I could not live here with another countess in residence," she pointed out reasonably.

"You are the only Countess of Standish now, Mother," he pointed out darkly.

"But that could change at any moment," Lady Standish countered hopefully. "But we digress from the matter at hand. You have isolated yourself far too much over the past two years, Victor. I tried to keep my opinion to myself on the subject, but it really is time for you to return to Society. You cannot be a hermit, you are the Earl of Standish."

"Does not being the Earl afford me the privilege to be whatever I want to be?"

"No, it does not, and well you know it. There are responsibilities that come attached to the title, and you have shirked them long enough. You are well past the age of receiving a lecture from your mama so I will try to cease, but see that you are in a proper frame of mind to welcome my guests on Tuesday. They will be arriving at seven. I have already spoken with Mrs. Hill about the preparations, so you need not trouble yourself. Just be ready to receive at the prescribed time."

"Yes, Mother," the earl answered in a chastened tone of voice that was belied by the amused twinkle in his eye.

Secretly, his mother was pleased to see that her haughty son was finding things more amusing these days, even if it was at her own expense. She decided she had done all she could for the time being and took her leave, prepared to fight this battle again another day.

Chapter Six

The earl had informed Felicia that Parliament would soon be dispersing for the summer and the household would be removing to his country estate, Standish, for a couple of months. She was aquiver with a myriad of emotions over the prospect. Change had become something to fear in her experience, and she had come to enjoy the routine she and Penelope had established. But while she was enjoying exploring the city with her young charge, she was a country girl at heart and looked forward to the clear air and vast vistas that would no doubt be had at Standish.

And then there was the earl himself. No doubt in the country he would be more accessible to his daughter and her governess. This thought filled Felicia with strange feelings of nervous energy. She was torn between longing for time spent with him and wanting to run from him whenever he turned up. It was a dilemma she pushed to the back of her mind time and again.

Penelope was looking forward to returning to her home in the country. She was excited to show her dear Felicia all her favourite places on the estate. And playing with her dogs would be so much fun!

Felicia had to struggle to maintain Penelope's attention as she kept remembering different things she wished to describe about the house, grounds, and stables on the estate.

"And the head groom is the very best, Felicia. His name is Irish, since he's from Ireland, and he always takes me riding whenever I feel like going." All of a sudden, she thought of a very important matter. "Oh my goodness, I forgot to ask you if you ride. You do ride, don't you, Felicia? My last governess was actually afraid of horses, if you can imagine. But you are the very best, and I am absolutely certain that you would not be so silly as to be afraid of horses."

Felicia laughed with delight over her charge's exclamations. "You are quite correct, my dear. I love horses, and I do enjoy riding. I have been out of practice for some time, but I trust the stables will have some gentle, old horse for me to use, and we shall have a lovely time. But now is not the time to be thinking of that. We shall be remaining in London for at least another week, possibly two, and you really must learn a few more things before we leave. Now please, reread that last paragraph as I am quite certain you do not recall a single word of it."

With a sheepish grin, Penelope returned her nose to her textbook. They continued working diligently for a few moments before they were again interrupted. Mary, their maid, was at the door.

"I'm right sorry to disturb you, miss, but his lordship is asking to see you. He said it's right urgent and for you to come straight away. I can sit with my lady while you go downstairs."

Felicia was startled by the summons and gazed at the maid with a degree of dismay. However, Penelope was not disturbed in the least. "Hurry up, Felicia, before we perish of curiosity. The sooner you go see what he wants, the sooner you can come and tell me."

Rolling her eyes in amusement, Felicia arose from her seat and made her way to the door before turning back to admonish Penelope. "Make sure you mind whatever Mary tells you and try to get to the end of the page before I get back."

"Yes, Miss," the student answered with sham humility.

With a tinkle of laughter, Felicia swept from the room and ran lightly down the stairs. The closer she got to the earl's library, the tighter her nerves became. *What could the earl want to discuss with me now? I hope all is well.* She worried as she stood outside his door, dithering before she finally tapped lightly.

"Enter," he summoned, his rich voice rumbling through the solid oak.

Felicia hesitated another moment before slowly pushing the door open and poking her head around it.

"Come in, please, Miss Scott. There is a rather important matter I need to discuss with you." Seeing her wide eyes and pale face, he hastened to add, "Have no fear, I am not about to ring a peal over you. On the contrary, we are most happy with your services. I am not about to lecture you, no matter what you have to say on the subject at hand."

Felicia relaxed marginally but still remained hovering near the door, causing the earl to laugh and beckon her further. "Come, have a seat. I have a feeling you will not wish to be standing for this conversation."

"If you are trying to set me at my ease, my lord, you are doing a rather dismal job of it," she muttered as she came and took a seat on the proffered chair, causing Victor to chuckle anew.

Lord Standish leaned back in his chair and gazed at the pretty young woman before him. He was actually nervous to broach the subject, but the necessity was brought on by the note he had just received from his mother.

"We have not really gotten to know one another very much despite the almost two months you have been in residence, have we, Miss Scott?"

Felicia blushed rosily and stumbled for an answer. "Not terribly well, I guess not, my lord. I am not at all mysterious, though. Was there anything in particular you wished to know?" She was bewildered about where he might be going with this conversation.

"As a matter of fact, I was wondering what sort of Society you associated with in the town you grew up in. Forgive me, Miss Scott, I do not at the moment recall what was the name of that town."

"Denbigh, my lord, near the county Flint."

"Quite right, Denbigh. Did your parents do much entertaining amongst the villagers?" Standish made every effort to curb his snobbery, but it was evident he did not think too highly of whatever socializing may have been done in Felicia's village.

Eyeing him askance, Felicia's face suffused with hot colour, but she answered with restrained dignity. "Since my father was merely a baron, we were not the highest members of Society in our village. The Viscount of Strath has an estate in the area, and he and his wife would host some sort of an event whenever they were in residence, to which my family would be invited. The village had assembly rooms in which country dances would often be held. The local squire would very often entertain, and my own parents dearly enjoyed hosting dinners or routs on occasion. I am quite certain none of these would be comparable to the entertainments on offer by your friends during the Season, but if you ever wished to visit Denbigh, you would have to be a very high stickler to find fault with the hospitality available to you."

Victor was ashamed to feel shocked over the list she had just named. *How did this gently bred female end up as governess in his house*? Of course, he knew the story of her circumstances, but it still boggled his mind that she could have fallen so far. While she was obviously not a member of the high *ton*, she was gentry, and as such, it was not in the realm of the ridiculous for her to answer his mother's request.

"Thank you for your honesty, Miss Scott. I wish to impose upon your kindness for a favour for my mother."

"Of course, my lord," she was quick to reply.

"You might wish to wait to find out what she requests before agreeing," he pointed out kindly.

"Your mother is a dear lady, and I would do whatever was in my power to accommodate her," Felicia vowed with commendable loyalty, causing the Earl to smile anew.

"You might be aware the countess is hosting a dinner party here this evening," he began, watching Felicia's brow furrow in concentration. "It turns out she has received a last minute cancellation, and her numbers are out. She requests your presence to even them out."

As he finished his explanation, Felicia's eyes widened in shock, and she began shaking her head in denial. "I now understand your question about Denbigh Society, my lord, but it has been quite some time since I attended any fine function. I am a governess, my lord. It is not fitting for me to eat at your dining table," she answered with proud dignity, coming to her feet and preparing to quit the room.

"Please, sit back down and think on the matter before you refuse. There is nothing unfitting about sharing a meal at my mother's request. You are not a servant, and you are gently born. There would be naught amiss were you to join my mother's party."

"Her other guests may not agree, my lord, no matter how progressive Lady Standish might be," she pointed out, a quaver evident in her voice.

The earl gazed steadily at Felicia, observing the rapid rise and fall of her breath and noting her ebbing colour. "I have a feeling it is not the question of your position that is causing you to demure. Tell me the truth, Miss Scott. You were born to this Society. You are fit to eat at my table. Why will you not dine with me?" As he spoke, his own convictions on the subject grew, and he was prepared to insist on the matter.

Felicia looked at the earl while tears gathered on her eyelashes. She willed them not to fall but was at a loss as to how to answer him. Once in her life it would have been a dream come true to be invited to dine with the likes of the Earl of Standish. Now, she was his governess and her dreams were much simpler. Having a roof over her head and regular meals was an answer to her prayers. She did not think it wise to alter the state of her aspirations.

But the crux of the matter was, "I have nothing to wear, my lord," she murmured shyly as he shouted with laughter.

"Despite being an absolutely perfect governess, at your heart, you are the same as every female—it comes down to the perfect gown."

Felicia blushed and shot him a disgruntled look.

"If that is truly your only concern, then we have no problem. I have yet to rid the house of my late wife's abundance of gowns. You are of a size with her, if memory serves me accurately. Mrs. Hill could show them to you, and you are welcome to take your pick of whichever suits your fancy."

"Oh no, my lord, I cannot do that," she protested weakly, although the very feminine side of her longed to dress up and sit with wellborn adults for an evening.

"Certainly you can, and you must if we are not to disappoint the countess," he cajoled bracingly, shamelessly using the one piece of leverage he knew he held.

Felicia continued to regard him steadily for a number of moments, visibly weighing all her options and struggling to make a sound decision.

Finally she concluded, "Very well, my lord, if you are sure it is acceptable." She paused for a moment then smiled sweetly. “Thank you for your kind invitation and offer of the use of a gown. What time should I be ready? I have to make sure Penelope is set for the evening. She might be distressed over the change to her routine.”

“She should be fine, but if it would make things easier for you, I could have a talk with her,” the Earl offered kindly.

Felicia grinned good-naturedly in response. “I should be able to manage, my lord, thank you.”

The Earl pulled the cord to summon the housekeeper before he thought to answer her question. “My mother’s guests are due to begin arriving at seven o’clock. Do you think you can manage to be ready by then?” he asked rather dubiously, remembering how long it would take his wife to prepare for evening events.

“It should be easy if your assessment of size is correct and no alterations are needed,” Felicia answered steadily, rising to her feet upon the housekeeper’s entrance.

“Mrs. Hill, please show Miss Scott to the room housing Lady Standish’s gowns. The countess has requested Miss Scott’s attendance at our dinner party this evening.”

Mrs. Hill grinned with delight but merely dropped a quick curtsy and a polite. "Yes, my lord," before exiting the room with Felicia in tow.

~~~

Once they were out of the earl's earshot, Mrs. Hill turned to Felicia with glee. "How very exciting, Miss. It will be so nice to see someone enjoying m'lady's gowns. She so loved to dress up in her finery and continued to buy new ones, even when she was too sick to wear them anywhere. Hurry along, deary, I can't wait to show you."

Felicia couldn't help laughing over the other woman's excitement. Luckily, it was contagious and she soon felt her nerves lessening and her own excitement over the evening rising. As they climbed the stairs, she thought of something. "Pardon me, Mrs. Hill. Would you mind terribly waiting for me for a quick moment? I was thinking Penelope would enjoy helping us pick what I should wear this evening since they *are* her mother's gowns."

"What a lovely idea, my dear. No, I don't mind waiting a'tall. You hurry upstairs and find the wee one. I'll just wait here for you to return."
~~~

Felicia dashed up the stairs and returned momentarily with Penelope and Mary hurrying along behind her.

"Oh Miss, thanks ever so for lettin' me join in the fun." The young maid, too, was excited over the prospect. "If you'd like, I could help you with your hair if you don't have a hand for it. Me sisters and I would always practice on each other. If you don't mind me sayin' so, I was right good at it."

"Thank you for your kind offer, Mary. I would appreciate the help. I would only be able to manage the simplest of styles on my own."

The maid blushed with delight while they all traipsed behind Mrs. Hill to a room adjacent to the master's bedchamber. It was not an overly large room, but when the housekeeper threw open the door, they saw the room was wall-to-wall full of sumptuous gowns in every shade of every colour and nearly every possible fabric. Felicia had to fight to keep her jaw from falling open in amazement.

Penelope said it best. "Oh dear," she whispered in hushed tones as they slowly entered the room. "How will you ever choose?"

"That is an excellent question. I do not even know where to start. There are just so many! But we must be quick since I only have a couple of hours, and I might need to make adjustments. Mrs. Hill, do you know if these gowns have been sorted into any type of order?"

"Yes, Miss, I believe they were hung in sections of which type of attire, so the evening gowns should be over here." The housekeeper matched her words to action and showed the governess where she should be looking.

"That's a relief. At least we don't have to look through everything. But this is still a rather large selection, and there is such a large assortment to pick from. I guess we could start by colour. Some of these are rather mature for me. So let us look at these lighter-coloured ones, and we'll see which style would best suit me."

Upon these words, Mary quickly jumped in to pull down the indicated items. They quickly narrowed their choice down to three, which Felicia then tried on to see which was the best fit.

The earl had actually been right. The dress they decided on was nearly a perfect fit with only very slight alterations needed to tuck in a couple of loose spots. The soft pink was flattering to Felicia's pale skin, and the high-waisted cut and deceptively demure neckline accentuated her figure that was usually well hidden under the serviceable brown frocks she favoured for her time with Penelope. Mary offered to do the necessary stitching, while Felicia ran back up to the nursery to spend a bit of time getting Penelope settled back into her routine before she rang for a footman to bring water for her bath.

The governess' room was not equipped with a good mirror, so Felicia was blissfully unaware of the drastic change in her appearance. Mary had been effusive in her compliments, but Felicia had brushed those off as pleasantries from a friend. Not having an egotistical shade to her personality, she was unprepared for the dazzlingly hot look in the earl's eyes as he watched her descending the last few steps into the foyer of his elegant house.

"My compliments, Miss Scott," he offered in marked understatement. "You shall be a remarkable addition to our dinner party this evening." Victor could barely tear his eyes from the refreshing beauty before him. He was deeply relieved when the knocker sounded and Alfred ushered in the first arrival.

Felicia smiled shyly at the countess as she breezed in past the butler, walking straight to her son's governess. "Felicia, my dear, I knew this would be a marvellous idea!" she declared without explanation. "Come into the morning room and receive guests with me."

Felicia was surprised and gratified to be introduced for the evening as "our dear friend, Miss Scott, visiting from Denbigh." No mention was made of her being Penelope's governess, and the other guests accepted her into their company without demur.

Chapter Seven

"Denbigh, did you say?" asked an aging debutante a year or two older than Felicia. "Are you acquainted with the Viscount of Strath?"

"Not very well. He and his wife are very hospitable and invited me and my family to their home on occasion, but they did not spend very much time in the area, so we did not become very well acquainted. Are you close with them?" Felicia asked innocently, unfamiliar with the games of the *ton*.

"Oh yes, we are friends," came the quick reply from Lady Gertrude.

"Oh good, I have been wondering how their little boy, Charles, has been faring since his bout of pneumonia this past spring, but I was uncomfortable presuming upon the connection. Do you know if he is fully recovered?"

Lady Gertrude blushed angrily as she had to admit that she had no idea how the boy fared. Evidently she was not such a close friend as she wished to present. The earl had witnessed the exchange and smiled in amusement before he took in Felicia's bewildered expression. His own expression softened in admiration of her lack of artifice. He thought to come to her aid, but the countess beat him to it.

"Come along, Felicia, you have not gotten acquainted with my dear friend, Lady Banting. She and I have been friends since our debut into Society. You will like her, I am certain." Felicia was happy to oblige. Lady Banting was a spirited, older lady with kind eyes. She took to Miss Scott at first introduction.

"Lady Standish tells me you are a recent orphan. Let me start by saying how sorry I am for your loss. Losing both parents at the same time and you not yet married, that is a tragedy, my dear."

Surprised by this unlooked for kindness, Felicia had to swallow past the lump that formed in her throat, while she blinked back the tears gathering in her wide, glistening eyes. It would not do to dissolve in a puddle of tears during her first high society function. Imagining the scene in her mind's eye got her past her grief, making her grin.

Felicia dropped another brief curtsy to the countess' friend. "It is so kind of you to say so, my lady. You are right, it is a tragedy, but I have been blessed with some good friends and a safe harbour in the storm." She then skilfully steered the conversation into less volatile waters. "Have you been in Town for the entire Season, Lady Banting?"

"Yes, my dear, my husband sits in the House of Lords for every last session. He does love his politics, my dear, so he insists on being in London almost constantly. We will be heading to our estate during the mass exodus, as will no doubt the earl's household. Will you be returning to Denbigh for the summer, Miss Scott?"

"Not this year, my lady." Felicia could sense the other lady's question was not motivated by any ill will, but it was still not a practical subject to discuss, if it were not to be revealed that she was the governess. She again steered the conversation elsewhere. "If I recall correctly, Lord Banting's estate is in the region of Yorkshire. I have not visited this area myself, but I have heard it is very beautiful. Do you farm anything in particular?"

It was exactly the perfect question as the Bantings were enthusiastic breeders of a particular strain of roses, and Lady Banting had plenty to say on the subject. Felicia managed to keep a polite smile and a look of interest upon her face until she was relieved to hear Lord Standish beside her.

"Alfred has just informed us that dinner is now being served. If you ladies would be so kind as to accompany me to the dining room, we can proceed."

He had been observing Felicia as unobtrusively as possible while she mingled with his guests and then as she became entrapped in conversation with Lady Banting. Her elegance and grace were as surprising to him as they were lovely to observe. He secretly hoped his mother had placed her sufficiently close to him at the table so he could continue to enjoy watching her experience her first foray into Society.

Victor was delighted to see that his private wish had been granted when they arrived in the dining room and examined the place cards. The earl, of course, was at the head of the table, but Felicia was only a couple of places away. It would rule out conversation between the two of them, but he would be able to overhear some of her conversations and keep a close eye on her throughout the meal.

As dinner progressed, Victor found it increasingly difficult to pay attention to the comments of those sitting closest to him. Why his mother had seen fit to place the most boring conversationalists closest to him, he would never be able to fathom. His eyes continued to be drawn with increasing frequency in his governess' direction. Clearly she was having no difficulty paying attention to her companions. Periodically, the sound of her soft chuckle would reach his ears, causing him to wish wholeheartedly that there were no other guests in his home. He was, of course, being unreasonable. If not for his mother's dinner party, he would never have witnessed this side of Miss Scott and would most likely never have shared a dinner table with her.

It was difficult for Victor to believe the dress she had on was one his wife had worn. If Penelope's mother had ever worn the frock, it had certainly not looked as good on her as it did on Felicia, he thought absently. That particular shade was a far sight prettier than the hideous shades of brown the young woman usually saw fit to wear, he thought rather harshly as he forced his eyes once more back to his plate and made a valiant effort to listen to the inanities being uttered by Lady Gertrude, who was seated on his left. It crossed Victor's mind whether his mother were trying to make a match between the lady and him. If she were, he thought crossly, she was far off the mark. The sour young woman was definitely not a candidate to be the next Countess of Standish.

Victor glanced down the table toward where his mother was sitting and was surprised to see a complacent smile upon her face. It looked as though the countess was vastly pleased with herself, although her son could not for the life of him fathom why. With a mental shrug, he absently thought he was glad she seemed to be enjoying herself since he certainly wasn't.

It was somewhere between the fish course and the beef that it struck the earl rather forcibly how much he would enjoy having Miss Scott at his dining table on a regular basis. It didn't take his agile mind long to leap from that thought to the realization that Miss Scott could actually be a candidate for the position of his next countess. It took considerable effort for Victor to contain his own reaction to this rash thought. He forced himself not to gaze at Felicia, not to even glance in her direction, until he had contained his rebellious thoughts.

Lady Gertrude blinked as the Earl of Standish grinned at her. "So you agree with my suggestion that you take me riding in Hyde Park tomorrow, my lord?"

"What?" Victor asked inelegantly. He had not been listening to a word she had been saying and was now surprised by her boldness. "Pardon me. That is to say, of course, I would be delighted," he countered lamely, wishing heartily that she were elsewhere or that he could somehow turn the tables on her. His earlier grin returned, although this time it had a slightly villainous twist to it as he thought of the perfect foil to her plot. He could almost look forward to the occasion.

He realized the look on his face must have revealed some of his calculating thoughts because Lady Gertrude blinked in surprise, and some of the delight over her clever entrapment of him dimmed as unease flickered across her face. But her discomfort did not last long, he observed, as she must have realized she had at least gained her objective and thus gave up on trying to converse with him, instead turning her attention to Mr. Sparks, who was seated to her left.

~~~

Lady Standish finally stood, signalling the time for the ladies to withdraw to allow the gentlemen their port. As they exited the room, the countess again engaged Felicia in conversation.

"Are you managing comfortably, my dear?"
~~~

"Oh, yes, my lady. I must admit I am enjoying myself far more than I had expected. I was a bundle of nerves when his lordship mentioned your invitation, but everyone has been quite lovely. And the dinner was an indescribable treat. I must compliment you on your choices, my lady. I have, of course, not attended an excessive number of high society meals, but this one far surpassed even that put on by the Viscountess of Strath, and she is reputed to be a terrible stickler when it comes to course selection."

The countess smiled in delight over Felicia's sincerity. "Oh, Felicia, my dear, you are a treasure. Now come and mingle a bit more. I do not think you have yet met my daughter. Isabella, allow me to introduce you to Miss Scott. Felicia, this is Isabella, Lady Derby. Her husband was called away to tend to an emergency on their estate so you will not be able to meet him tonight, but he is the Viscount of Dartmouth."

Felicia was surprised that no one had mentioned Penelope's aunt before now, but she kept this to herself as she curtsied to the beautiful, raven-haired young woman before her. There was clearly a rather large gap in age between the earl and his sister. She looked nothing like Victor, and it became obvious she was of a different temperament as well when she giggled through the introduction.

“Oh, Miss Scott, I am delighted to make your acquaintance. I am always so happy to meet the objects of my mama’s matchmaking efforts.”

“Hush, Bella, do not tease,” Lady Standish admonished.

Lady Derby blushed becomingly as she turned wide, innocent eyes toward Felicia. “Oops, was I not supposed to mention that? Pray forgive me, Miss Scott.”

Felicia was momentarily confused by this inexplicable exchange, but Isabella’s social chatter quickly distracted her for the next several moments. Lady Derby was the epitome of a social butterfly. Felicia had no doubt she had been highly popular as a debutante; she was pretty as a picture and seemed untroubled by any overly intellectual thoughts. During the ten minutes she conversed with Felicia, she flitted from one light subject to the next.

“Miss Scott, that gown is absolutely ravishing, I must say. It is the perfect shade for your complexion. And the cut is so perfectly complimentary to your figure. You absolutely must tell me who makes your gowns.”

Felicia could not help smiling over the young lady's exclamations, despite her discomfort with the direction the conversation had taken. It was obvious to her that the flighty young woman had no idea that Felicia was her niece's governess. Glancing down at the beautiful, but borrowed, dress she was wearing, she mustered a rueful smile.

"I must apologize, Lady Isabella. I do not at this moment recall where this particular frock came from. If you are really wishing to know, I could probably ask my abigail. She no doubt keeps better track of these details than I do."

"Oh no, I am sure it is of no matter." Seeing her brother approaching, she gave him a jaunty smile before excusing herself. "It was lovely to make your acquaintance, Miss Scott. You must call on me at your earliest convenience. I am certain we shall become fast friends. But I really must speak to Lady Banting before she takes her leave." With that final exclamation she whirled on her heel and departed in a cloud of perfume, leaving Felicia feeling a trifle dazed.

"That was a very diplomatic answer, Miss Scott."

Felicia felt a shiver thrill down her spine at hearing the earl's deep voice low in her ear. Maintaining her composure with a bit of an effort, she turned to him with a questioning look. "Whatever do you mean, my lord?"

"You cannot recall which dressmaker your frock is from?" he asked dryly, smiling over her heightened blush.

Felicia shrugged. "Well, it was not an untruth."

"Perhaps the first half was not, but I am quite certain your abigail would not be privy to the information either."

Felicia could not help smiling over the unaccustomed teasing from the earl. It was a rarity to see the earl in anything other than a serious mood.

"You seem to be enjoying your evening, my lord," she commented.

"As do you, Miss Scott. Are you glad you accepted my mother's invitation?"

"Was it an invitation, my lord? You managed to somehow turn it into a command." Felicia had meant this to be another tease and was unprepared for his reaction.

Looking contrite, he began to apologize. "I am so sorry, Miss Scott. I can be terribly highhanded, I must admit. I hope it has not been a terrible imposition."

She could not suppress the surprised laughter this invoked. "Oh yes, my lord, it was a terrible imposition to dress up in a beautiful gown and eat a scrumptious meal with interesting company. I hardly know if I shall survive the experience." Her eyes were dancing with mirth as she put a delicate hand dramatically to her forehead as though to prevent a faint.

"Impudent chit," Victor admonished with an answering twinkle before he forced himself to move on to other guests, lest he draw too much attention to the two of them.

As the rest of the evening quickly passed in a whirl of conversation, Felicia became a bit uncomfortable wondering if she should at some point excuse herself. She was embarrassed to ask either the earl or his mother, shy to reveal her innocent lack of experience. She chided herself for being missish. This was a particularly peculiar situation. No doubt there was not an overabundance of rules as to when the visiting miss should turn back into the governess.

Since no one seemed to be looking askance at her, she ended up remaining with Lady Standish until the last of the guests had bidden farewell.

With a sigh of contentment, Lady Standish settled herself on the settee after Alfred promised to return with a cup of tea for her.

"Well, Miss Scott, I thank you for accommodating me this evening. You were a delightful addition to my little party."

"Thank you, my lady. I was honoured to be included."

"It is rather a shame you are Penelope's governess," Lady Standish mused. "You were such a hit with my guests. I would love to take you around with me as I make my calls. I have not had a young companion since Isabella got married. And actually, even before that she was not nearly as accommodating as you are, my dear. I guess daughters do not wish to be tied to their mama's side any more than sons do," she concluded rather wistfully, with a sidewise glance at Victor, who was silently witnessing the exchange.

Felicia had no idea how to answer the countess' comment. Shame or not, she *was* Penelope's governess, and quite happy she was to have the position. Being Lady Standish's friend would not keep a roof over her head, but she *had* enjoyed the evening and had no wish to offend the older lady. Rather helplessly, she glanced at the earl and was momentarily shocked senseless by the intense look upon his face as he watched her. Blinking to clear her inertia, she felt her eyebrows inching higher on her forehead as she puzzled through what he could possibly be thinking. Blessedly, she was not kept long in the dark as he began to speak.

“Miss Scott cannot accompany you on your calls tomorrow, Mother. She and Penelope will be riding with me in the park after Pen’s lessons are done.” Victor stated this as nonchalantly as possible, awaiting reaction from his audience.

Felicia strived for no reaction, which was a nearly impossible feat when her jaw was wishing to drop toward the floor. She blinked rather owlishly at him, but managed to keep a serene smile on her face. She hoped the countess could not ascertain from looking at her that this was the first she was hearing of the outing. With a mental shrug, she thought this was perhaps normal behaviour if a lord wished to spend time with his daughter. She was soon corrected.

“And why will Miss Scott be riding with you in the Park, my lord?” his mother asked, her eyebrows furrowing in consternation.

“Because in a moment of inattention I was tricked into agreeing to take Lady Gertrude for a ride in Hyde Park.” Victor shook his head in wry dismay over how that folly could have possibly taken place, while his mother tried to hide her secret smile of satisfaction. Victor saw the smile and misunderstood. “If you are trying to make a match between me and Lady Gertrude, you can rethink that plan immediately, my lady. I can assure you she is in no way an appropriate candidate to be the next countess."

Curious as to his thought processes and not wishing to reveal her true thoughts, Lady Standish questioned further. "What could possibly make her inappropriate? She is well bred, of a good family, and moves in similar circles as you. I think she would make a fine countess."

"Perhaps," Victor allowed, "but for some other earl, not this one."

The relief that surged through Felicia at hearing how adamant he was on this particular subject took her aback. She really had no business caring who he might consider as his future bride. But that being said, she herself was adamant that Lady Gertrude would be neither a good mate for him, nor an acceptable stepmother for Penelope.

Lady Standish merely smiled benignly. "Very well, my darling son. Thank you again for allowing me to have my little party here."

The earl barely managed to stop from rolling his eyes. "I told you, you are welcome to use any of our properties whenever you so wish."

The countess smiled almost cheekily. "In that case, I would be happy to have another one. When do you plan to remove to Standish?"

Victor allowed his eyes to stray toward Felicia, as though seeking her confirmation.

Felicia's lips parted, as though to answer, and Victor's gaze sharpened intently. Felicia caught herself, reminding herself once more that she was merely the governess; it was not her place to remind the earl when he planned to leave London. She smiled encouragingly at him. Victor blinked, and it became obvious that he did not remember the question.

The countess controlled her gleeful smile as she stood. "Well, never mind. We can discuss it when I come for a visit with my granddaughter. You two have a pleasant night." She gracefully swept from the room, leaving a heavy silence in her wake.

Uncomfortable to be left alone with the earl, Felicia, too, stood to take her leave. "Thank you, my lord, for the use of this lovely gown. We ensured that the few necessary adjustments are removable. I shall return it to that room as soon as it has been laundered."

"There is absolutely no need to return it. Please, it is yours. I can assure you I have no need for a lady's gown," he concluded with a wry chuckle as he saw she was about to protest.

Felicia was uncomfortable accepting such a personal gift, but saw the sense in what he said. Unable to put words to her disquiet, she merely accepted as graciously as possible. "Thank you, my lord, that is very generous."

There was another moment of silence while Victor continued looking at her quizzically. Felicia again filled the silence. "You mentioned, my lord, that you wish for Lady Penelope and me to accompany you as you escort Lady Gertrude. What time should we be ready to depart?"

"Do you not think you could see your way free to call me Victor, at least when we are not in company?" he asked rather plaintively, apropos of nothing.

Felicia blushed fiercely. "No, my lord, I could not! That would be most inappropriate."

Victor smiled at her endearingly, but allowed it to pass for the moment. "I promised Lady Gertrude we would pick her up at five o'clock, so it would be best if you and Pen could be ready at a quarter to, if that is acceptable to you."

"Yes, my lord," she answered stiltedly, still embarrassed over his request, and unable to look him in the eye.

"And one other thing, Felicia," he continued, using her name almost tauntingly. "I do not think I could bear to see you return to those hideous browns you seem to favour after seeing you so becomingly attired this evening. Would you be so kind as to dig through the dresses and find something appropriate for riding?"

Now Felicia's eyes flew to his once more. He thought her face must hurt, so fiery was her blush.

"My lord, I do not think, that is to say, I hardly see…" She broke off in confusion.

"There is nothing inappropriate in this request, Felicia. I wish it. Please, see that it is done." He reverted to haughtiness in order to get his way.

"Very well, my lord," she agreed quietly before turning on her heel and nearly fleeing the room with a barely audible, "Good night, my lord," lingering on the air in her wake.

Victor was left standing alone looking at the doorway, his smile almost that of a love struck youth rather than a mature lord of the realm. He had to chuckle at his own expense as the butler came in and started upon seeing him standing there.

"Are you all right, my lord?" Alfred asked solicitously, looking at him with puzzlement.

"I am perfectly fit, Alfred. Thank you for asking. I shall be in my library for a time before retiring. Feel free to take yourself off to your own bed after you lock up. I can get myself settled on my own."

"If you are certain, my lord, I will thank you."

"Good night, Alfred."

Alfred was struck almost speechless. The earl was never a harsh master, but he had rarely shown an interest in his servants' feelings. He grinned at the earl before wishing him a good night as well.

Chapter Eight

The next morning, Felicia felt nervous and excited and just a wee bit queasy. She tried not to allow any of it to show. There was no way Penelope would get any studying done if she knew what they would be up to that afternoon. Felicia figured Mary would not be able to keep it to herself either, so she left Mary to watch over their student while she went by herself to the very large dressing room.

She was rummaging around near the back of the room, head and shoulders into a crate full of ribbons, bows, and all sorts of unmentionables. So focused on her search was she, that she was blissfully unaware of her audience until he spoke.

"You are nothing like her, you know. I wonder if that is why I find you so utterly fascinating," Victor mused before grinning in delight over her shriek of terror.

"Oh, my lord, you fairly scared the breath out of me," Felicia declared with a nervously trembling hand placed over her racing heart.

"I do apologize, Felicia. I did not realize you were quite so absorbed. Perhaps you *are* like her."

"Like who, my lord?" Felicia asked, puzzled over his demeanour. It crossed her mind to wonder if the earl drank to excess, so erratic had his behaviour been of late.

"My late countess," he stated rather baldly. "Don't get me wrong, she was a sweet little lady. But her gowns and her friends were the most important things in the whole world to her. They were more important than the baby, and certainly *much* more important than me. This selection of frocks is actually only a fraction of what she had. They are just the ones I have yet to dispose of."

Felicia looked at him in disbelief. "Surely you are jesting with me, my lord. How could she have possibly had more? Of what use would even more be?"

Victor's distracted look dissolved into a grin. "There you go. You just proved that you really are very different from her."

Felicia was not quite sure what to make of the earl in this mood, nor did she know how to respond to his comparison of her and his dead wife. But he was looking at her expectantly, so she launched into speech with a question.

"If you don't mind my prying, what happened to her, my lord? Penelope never speaks of her, so I assumed it has been a long time since she passed."

"Why can you not call me Victor?" he asked almost plaintively, before answering her question without allowing her time to answer his. "It has been eighteen months since she died, but she was ill for several months before that. She refused to acknowledge her illness for quite a while, kept up all her social activities until she collapsed one day. Finally, she allowed me to send for a physician, but by then there was nothing that could be done. Of course, there is no saying if anyone could have done anything for her had she seen a doctor sooner, but a part of me has yet to forgive her for that."

"Oh dear, surely you know it was not her fault. Perhaps she was afraid of what was happening to her. She must have been quite young. No doubt she thought nothing bad could possibly happen to her at such a young age and with such a privileged position." She spoke in such kind, convincing tones that the earl was soothed momentarily.

"Do you always see the good in everything?" he asked querulously after a moment of reflection.

"Well, in this particular case, it is easy for me to do so since I was not emotionally involved in the situation," she answered almost apologetically.

"Perhaps you are correct about her. Maybe it is just one of those strange aberrations. But it is so much easier to cope with when there is someone to blame."

"Did you love her very much?" Felicia dared to ask, her voice barely above a whisper.

"Sadly, no. I think that is part of why I have been so angry at her dying on me. I always hoped that with time she would grow up and be the wife and mother I thought she was capable of being. Now I have a motherless daughter on my hands."

They stood there gazing at each other pensively for a moment before the earl broke the spell that held them.

"Did you manage to find more gowns for your use? I hesitate to point it out, but I cannot help noticing you are wearing one of those hideous brown frocks I remember quite expressly wishing to never see again."

Felicia let out a tinkle of pleasing laughter. "Oh my lord, you are too droll. This frock is far from hideous, although I have to admit in comparison to anything in this room, it does fade into insignificance. And I do recall you requesting not to have to see it, but if I could be so bold, I did not think to see you until the appointed hour of quarter to five. As well, it would not do to wear an evening gown about the house—surely your staff would think I had run mad. But yes, I have found a few things that will be perfect for my use if you still have a mind to lend them to me."

"The entire contents of this room are yours to do with as you please," Victor declared grandly, making Felicia's eyes grow wide.

"These shall do me just fine for now, thank you, my lord. Now if you shall excuse me, I should return to the schoolroom." With her arms full of fabrics, Felicia hurried from the room, leaving the earl to contemplate his afternoon.

~~~

After returning to the nursery wing, Felicia felt as though the day were three times longer than usual. Every time she checked the clock, she was appalled to see how few minutes had gone by since her previous glance. While she dreaded seeing the horrendously haughty Lady Gertrude again, she figured it was a small enough price to pay for an afternoon spent in the earl's company.
~~~

Finally, the appointed time had come. Felicia felt like Cinderella with her lovely new clothes covering the fact that she was, in fact, just the governess. She clung tightly to Penelope's hand as they descended the stairs.

"Isn't this the most exciting adventure, Felicia?" Penelope asked with a grin. "Papa has never taken me for a ride in the park. Do you think we shall be riding in his phaeton?" The little girl jumped from step to step in her excitement.

"Don't get your hopes up about that, my dear. We will be four people, including Lady Gertrude, so I do not think we would all be able to squeeze into a phaeton. No doubt we will be riding in either a landau or a carriage."

Penelope wrinkled her nose at this news. "Who is Lady Gertrude?"

"She was a guest at your grandmother's dinner party last evening. Your papa invited her to go for a drive in the Park, and then he thought we would like to join them."

"I think it would be much better if it was just us with Papa," Penelope declared rather stubbornly.

"I might have to agree with you, my pet," answered the earl, making both girls start in surprise.

Felicia shot him a censorious look before turning back to Penelope. "When we receive an invitation, we cannot make stipulations as to who else is invited. I am quite sure you shall enjoy meeting Lady Gertrude. It shall be a good experience for us all."

Penelope didn't look completely convinced, but she didn't say anything further. Victor quirked his eyebrows quizzically at Felicia, but he, too, refrained from comment. Felicia was getting a bad feeling about how the afternoon was going to progress.

~~~

When Lord Standish escorted Lady Gertrude to his waiting carriage, it was obvious to its occupants she had not been warned there would be company with them on their ride. She shot daggers at Felicia and Penelope, but was all smiles when she turned back to the earl.

"How lovely that I get to meet your daughter, my lord," she simpered.

"Lady Gertrude, this is my daughter, Penelope," he introduced, as Penelope acknowledged the introduction, but with little enthusiasm. "And you remember Miss Scott from last night, I'm sure."
~~~

"How do you do?" Felicia murmured demurely, her eyes dancing with hidden mirth as she realized the earl's ploy. Remembering the discussion she had been almost too tired to pay attention to last night, she now saw that she and Penelope were to be a shield to protect him from the lady's advances.

Victor saw her amusement and was warmed by it.

Lady Gertrude all but ignored Felicia, but made an effort to converse with Penelope. "Are you enjoying your studies, Penelope? Have you been learning your letters?"

Penelope did love an audience, so she launched into a lengthy speech about all that she had been learning, as well as the various excursions she and Felicia had made of late. Felicia was watching her young charge with a charming level of interest, while Lady Gertrude could barely sit still, she was so bored. She suddenly broke in and interrupted Penelope with a sardonic laugh.

"Penelope, you make Miss Scott sound as though she is your governess. Why have you been so much in her company?"

"But she is my governess," Penelope answered in confusion.

Lady Gertrude turned to the earl in high dudgeon. "You had us dine with your daughter's governess?" she asked in some horror.

"Do not be vulgar, Lady Gertrude, it is not such a rare occurrence."

"Perhaps not, but you and your mother tried to pass her off as a well-born friend of the family," Gertrude argued.

"She *is* a well-born friend of my family. We did not lie," argued Victor, all semblance of pleasantness gone from his demeanour.

Unable to argue successfully with him, Gertrude turned her ire upon Felicia. "Why are you dressed in the first stare of fashion if you are the governess? You are not trying to snare a wealthy husband in the parson's mousetrap are you, Miss Scott?"

Felicia had no ready answer, feeling humiliated by her insinuations. Seeing her distress, Victor acted rashly.

"Do not speak with such disrespect to the future Countess of Standish, Lady Gertrude."

Silence fell upon all occupants of the carriage as all three females turned to him with widely varying reactions.

"Truly, Papa? Oh, this is just grand! Felicia, you told me my father might wish to remarry one day, but I had no idea it could be you. Why did you not tell me?" The little girl hugged Felicia to her in delight, while Felicia struggled for composure.

Lady Gertrude lost her struggle for composure. "You cannot be serious, my lord," she declared shrilly. "The Earl of Standish cannot marry his daughter's governess."

"Yes he can, and he will," Victor declared staunchly, although he was eyeing Felicia worriedly.

"Take me home this instant. I will not be a party to this travesty," Gertrude declared as tears of rage began to track down her cheeks.

Seemingly oblivious to Lady Gertrude's distress, Penelope was bouncing in her seat, peppering Felicia with questions. "When will you be married? Will that make you my mama? Does Grandmother know? Can I have a puppy?"

This last question was almost enough to make Felicia smile, but she merely patted Penelope's hand rather weakly before urging her to, "Hush, Pen, we shall discuss it all later."

The rest of the blessedly short ride passed in strained silence. Victor was silently berating himself as an unintelligent buffoon. He argued regularly and eloquently in the House of Lords, but he could not manage to declare himself without an irate audience. If only he'd had the presence of mind to anticipate Lady Gertrude discovering Felicia's position in the household, he could have been prepared to handle it with a degree more finesse. Now he wondered if he would ever be able to convince Felicia that he had been in earnest.

From the look on her face, Victor surmised that she was worrying over Gertrude's words, that she was somehow to blame. He longed to reassure her, but decided that any further discussion on the subject would most definitely be best left until they had a degree of privacy.

Gertrude continued to sniffle inelegantly until they pulled up outside her house. She scrambled down before the footman had properly let down the step, and she stalked off in a huff without a backward glance.

As soon as she was gone, Penelope hurled herself into her father's lap. "Did you mean it, or were you just trying to make that awful lady be quiet?" Penelope uttered the words that were running wildly through Felicia's mind.

Victor answered his daughter's question while looking steadily into Felicia's tear-filled eyes. "I meant every word, sweet pea."

"Oh goody!" Penelope resumed her bouncing, oblivious to the turmoil experienced by the adult occupants of the carriage.

As they pulled up in front of their own address, the earl helped his daughter alight and then advised her, "You run along with Mrs. Hill, my dear. Felicia and I have a few things we need to discuss."

Felicia had maintained her silence for a worrying length of time, and Victor was anxious to get her to his library where they could speak in peace. She had managed to prevent the tears shimmering in her eyes from spilling until she heard the click of the door, at which point she launched into speech as they spilled over and ran down her cheeks.

"Oh, my lord, why did you say something so rash? How will you ever extricate yourself from this situation? You can be sure the nasty Lady Gertrude will not keep silent on the matter."

"I have no wish to extricate myself from the situation. While it is, no doubt, the least romantic proposal in history, I stand by my words. You are the next Countess of Standish."

Felicia looked at him blankly for a moment. "But she was right. You cannot marry your daughter's governess. It just isn't done, my lord."

"I really do think that by now you must be able to call me by my given name."

Felicia managed a watery chuckle despite shaking her head. "My lord, you must see reason."

"I do see reason. You shall be a most excellent countess."

Felicia now thought of another wild possibility. "Are you trying to pinch pennies, my lord? Do you think to avoid paying my salary by making me your wife?"

Now it was the earl's turn to chuckle. "Do you really think I am that much of a simpleton, my dear? Surely you have noticed that countesses are far more expensive than governesses." Victor managed to gain possession of Felicia's hands and stop them from their wringing before he continued. "You brought light into this house that I don't think has ever been here."

Felicia's tears were drying up, and she listened to his words attentively. Joy and hope, which she had been studiously holding at bay, began to well in her breast, but she strove for reason. "But I can remain in the household as Penelope's governess. You needn't marry me in order to keep me here. I had no thought of leaving."

"That shan't be sufficient for me, my dear. Quite simply, I find that I cannot possibly live without you. Please say that you will marry me and make me feel whole."

Felicia stared at him quite seriously for one moment before throwing herself into his arms with a whoop of joy. She welcomed his warm embrace with her own innocent enthusiasm.

The End

Enjoyed this sweet story?
Don't miss out on Book 2:

The Debutante Bride

First comes marriage, then comes love.

Miss Elizabeth Dunseith grew up in genteel poverty, happy despite her abusive father and weak mother. The marriage her father has arranged for her seems shady, but despite her fears for her future, Beth is relieved to get away from home with her handsome, new husband.

Justin Fulton, Earl of Westfield, is puzzled by the contradictory behavior of his purchased bride. One moment she is haughty and cool, the next she is warm and endearing.

Their relationship is just starting to develop when Justin's meddling sister throws them off course and an old friend of Beth's complicates matters further.

Can their differences get sorted before it's too late to claim their happily ever after?

Another book series you will enjoy:

Mayfair Mayhem

Book 1

The Duke Conspiracy

Anything is possible with a spying debutante, a duke, and a conspiracy.

Rose is finding the Season to be a dead bore. She'd rather be helping her father with his diplomatic duties. Things become a little more interesting when she overhears details of a plot against her childhood friend and neighbor, the new Duke of Wrentham.

A family feud tore their friendship apart and now the duke, Alexander Milton, is uptight and proper and he has no room in his life for his old friend.

It soon becomes clear that a nefarious conspiracy is afoot - one that puts not only Alex's freedom in danger, but Rose's life.

Can they overcome all that stands between them? Or will their second chance at love be snuffed out before it can even truly begin?

A must read:

The Bequest Book Series

Book 1

Inheriting Trouble

The inheritance was meant to better her life, not muddle it.

It was only supposed to be a two week adventure, a vacation from her regular life in the village, but when Georgia gets to London, she meets the Earl of Crossley and sparks fly.

Confusion of identities force them together but cause conflict and controversy. It will take forgiveness and understanding on both their parts to reach a happily ever after.

About the Author

Wendy May Andrews has been reading whatever she could get her hands on since the age of five. She has been writing for almost as long but hasn't been sharing those stories with anyone but her mother until recently. Wendy lives in Toronto with her own real-life hero. When not writing or reading, they love to travel wherever the mood takes them.

༄ ༅

If you enjoyed this story, please leave me a review and follow me on amazon.com

We can also stay in touch on

My website:

wendymayandrews.com

Instagram:

www.instagram.com/WendyMayAndrews

Facebook:

www.facebook.com/WendyMayAndrews

Twitter:

twitter.com/WendyMayAndrews

Printed in Great Britain
by Amazon

33109620R00078